H O O T S

ONORABLE **R**DER **F** **H**E **O**URCE

To Victoria
So nice to meet you,
enjoy reading —
Martha Lanser

MARTHA LANSER

Printed and bound in the United States of America

First Printing, 2015

ISBN: 978-1-63192-812-3

Publisher, printer and distributor:

BookBaby
7905 N Crescent Blvd.
Pennsauken, NJ 08110

Ⅱ\ **bookbaby**

ACKNOWLEDGMENTS

Most of all I would like to thank my daughter, Sally Siebe, for her untiring help in many ways. She has spent many hours as my computer expert and collaborator in all phases of writing from when I first started revising my original story, to the final stages of publication. Larry Siebe also deserves a thank you for his patience and cooperation while Sally was away from home while spending time working with me.

I would like to thank Dr. Gregg Sartorius in his editing expertise and comments. Thanks goes also to Judy Zerillo for her science fiction teaching background, time spent reading and correcting when needed, as well as her generous encouragement when she said she thought my story was "awesome."

Special thanks to my husband, Edward Lanser, for his patient listening and sharing of ideas when I needed new insights in the development of my book.

Finally, I want to thank all those who read my book and make my writing worthwhile.

Martha Lanser

READER'S COMMENTS

In this science fiction spoof, Martha (Withington) Lanser captures the reader's attention as Commander Lance Locke struggles with his sense of duty to the Honorable Order Of The Source (HOOTS) and his romantic interludes with Celestia, the girl of his dreams. Although he is compelled to save the Hybridites from certain doom, Celestia's relentless pursuit allows her to find a way to not only save the Commander, but to gain his eternal love once and for all. For science fiction lovers, this story is one you cannot put down once you begin to see the plot unfold.

Dr. Gregg S. Sartorius

INTRODUCTION

Two main groups of beings occupy the earth. No records of their past are available after a great cataclysm occurred; both groups claim to be the original inhabitants. A technologically advanced group of beings are called Hybridites; they occupy Jameripan, the capitol of which is California Island. The Hybridites are unaware that their president is evil. In order to keep the ever-growing population in control, President Zarno plans to send space station XRZ29B, Captain Lance L. Locke in command, and a multitude of innocent Hybridites, into a black hole.

President Zarno is foiled by Lance's heroism. In order to avoid suspicion regarding his heartless scheme, Zarno publicly promotes Lance to Commander. Then, to get rid of Lance, a new plan is devised by Zarno. He convinces the public that a huge meteor will destroy the earth, so they must find a new planet to occupy. Zarno decides to send the unsuspecting loyal Commander on a mission to another galaxy, thereby getting rid of him once and for all.

Lance and his fiancée, Celestia Stevens, have a lovers quarrel. She is a scientist, torn between serving her country and making up with her lover before he leaves for his top-secret training mission. Celestia's employer, Dr. Noah T. Hall, discovers how to clone a monkey. Unable to leave her work, Celestia secretly clones herself so she can be in two places at once. Problems arise when her clone, Excella, also falls in love with Lance.

The other group, living on earth after the cataclysm, occupies Egyptralia. They are called Barbarians by the Hybridites. The Barbarians, although they have the ability of speech, are considered to be an advanced type of animal compared to the technologically

ix

advanced Hybridites. The Barbarians reproduce physically, while the Hybridites reproduce by cell replication. They also eat meat while the Hybridites eat various products produced in biospheres. The Barbarians are shuttled from their desert modest homes in Egyptalia to work like slaves in the Hybridite's biospheres, factories and service positions.

Alex Carter Taylor is a Barbarian archeologist. He works to help the 'Old Ones' who insist there is evidence of their heritage buried beneath the sands. When Alex makes a discovery, he tries to make a friendly Hybridite, Lance, see through the evil ruler Zarno and his corrupt government. The Honorable Order Of The Source (HOOTS) is a Sci-Fi containing action, adventure, romance and a little tongue-in-cheek humor.

CHAPTERS

CHAPTER I

SPACE

A sudden jolt wakened Captain Lance Locke from a sound sleep. Space station XRZ29B turned like a giant merry-go-round. At first he thought he was dreaming, but another jolt and the blaring emergency alarms brought him to his senses. From his bed, Captain Locke attempted to communicate with the command crew, but couldn't get through. After several more attempts he reluctantly threw off the covers, pulled on his boots, grabbed yesterdays uniform which was draped over a nearby chair, and dressed as quickly as possible. He was proud to put on his uniform. The emblem of an owl on the sleeve representing The Honorable Order Of The Source gave him a special sense of honor. This was no time to think about honor, however, it was simply a time for action. With one arm in a sleeve and his shirt only half on, he rushed from his quarters into the frenetic hallway. The incessant alert warnings and clanging alarms sounded even louder than when he was behind the closed door. The space station was a city in turmoil; it shook like the combination of a dizzying earthquake and the rocking of an ocean vessel in a hurricane.

Lance made his way down the tilting floor of the hallway, bumping into the wall on one side, and then the other, until he reached an open crowded mall area, where the shops and restaurants were always open. Since there was no sunrise or sunset as on earth, artificial lighting was perpetual in public places. The Hybridites could choose their own day or night hours, so many had been shopping or enjoying a meal in one of the restaurants. Lights were going on and off intermittently as the frantic inhabitants tried to maintain their equilibrium. Although the buildings within the space station had been sturdily built, the once carefully stocked goods and displays in the shops were not fastened down. Items were shaken from shelves and were being scattered every which way. Bottles crashed on floors, leaking slippery liquid onto walkways. Chairs and other moveable objects slid out from open shops as if they were on a tilt-a-wheel. Some Hybridites scrambled to stay on their feet as they sought to find a more stable area, while others desperately tried to hold onto railings or anything they could cling to or lock their fingers on.

Amid the crowd of panic-stricken Hybridites, Lance struggled to dodge people and objects as they flew about the open space. He ignored the heart-rending cries for help in order to reach the control tower as quickly as possible . . . that is, until he saw a mother striving to reach her baby that had slid some distance from her arms during the tremors. "My baby, my baby!" she frantically cried as she slid in the mess of slippery liquids and shattered glass. Concerned that those who were rushing to safety might trample the baby, Lance quickly grabbed the infant and gently placed her in the teary-eyed, grateful mother's arms before hurrying on to the control tower. It was evident that Lance's considerable strength was not diminished by his compassion.

The control tower was located at the center of the huge space complex, which was built as a way-station for earthling Hybridites hoping to find a new home in the universe for their burgeoning population. There were many sub-control areas throughout the space station that were needed to manage the intricate workings of such a gigantic complex. However, the least amount of turbulence was always strongest at the center station, and there the motion was enough to overcome even the hardiest of shipmates. The innermost control station housed a dome of screens, and equipment with panels that were going haywire with screaming alarms and flashing lights. Four men and one woman were seated at the controls desperately striving to steady the ship. This crew of pilots normally worked together harmoniously; but now, amid the stress and havoc, fear threw off their cooperation. Three of the men began shouting directions at each other, and most often at Stellar Odin, who sat at the main controls. Stellar was a young inexperienced pilot, who sat behind the main controls. He was a newcomer to the crew, and the other men didn't let him forget that by the way they challenged and belittled him. Their orders were confusing Stellar as each of the other men shouted at him from a different direction. Not only did they want to get the space station back to normal, they wanted to impress Surealia, the only female crewmember. Surealia was a very capable pilot. She was also a beauty by Hybridite standards and had a voice and a walk enhanced by her come-hither manner that was irresistible to the male Hybridites. It was easy to see why she attracted a lot of attention. In spite of her stunning beauty, she took her work very seriously. She worked quietly at her station trying everything she could think of to get the space station under control. While Stellar frantically attempted to do what he thought he should do, the other men continued to bark orders back and forth. "Pressure starboard, lift!" shouted one of them. Another yelled, "Pressure port side!" The third man confidently screamed, "Rockets upward, now down!" When their orders were directed at Stellar, he innocently tried his best to follow them, but it was obvious that he was beginning to panic under the pressure. "It's no use!" he shouted. . . . "We can't hold her back! If we get any closer it'll be too late . . . we'll be sucked in!"

Cries rang out from the crew as the reeling metropolis approached a point of no return. If they weren't able to keep back a certain distance from the edge of the gaping black abyss looming before them, there would be no way to break free. No one knew what would happen if they were sucked into the magnetic pathway of the black hole. Suddenly, Lance burst into the control station. "Increase power to the boosters!" he ordered as he replaced Stellar from his seat at the main controls. As he took command he added, "Steady . . . steady . . . okay, now more power!"

"You'll blow us apart!" Stellar yelled in defiance of his humiliating replacement.

Lance ignored his comments. "Ease to the right," he ordered. "A little more . . . more, that's it, slowly . . . but keep it going. Keep the power up!" Lance continued directing until XRZ29B leveled off. Then, it began vibrating with a violent shudder.

"This whole place will fly to pieces!" Stellar warned defiantly. "Better to take our chances in the black hole than to be scattered like toothpicks all over the universe!" Lance continued to ignore Stellar's warning, which made Stellar feel even more useless.

Everywhere except in the very center of the space station, the Hybridites were ripped loose from where they clutched at railings, posts or anything within reach. They dodged falling boxes and objects in stores or slipped on liquid and slid into walls, with furniture and other objects flying at them like projectiles. When the vibrating finally stopped, the stunned voyagers tried to regain their senses. Just as they thought the worst was over there was a sudden jolt, then another and another. The craft turned slightly to one side, and then veered backward just enough to keep from being sucked into the oblivion-threatening black hole. Wondrously, space station XRZ29B steadily leveled and floated effortlessly to its designated path as if nothing had ever happened.

The disoriented and relieved Hybridites picked themselves up from the rubble. The miracle was celebrated as the space ship regained stability. Strangers hugged one another, and mothers comforted crying children. Others wiped tears from the faces of those who had given up. It was clear to everyone that it was Captain Lance Locke who had taken control of the spacecraft city and was responsible for saving their lives. As the Hybridites gathered around Lance to celebrate his success and express their collective gratitude, the woman whose baby he had saved made her way to join the revelers. Looking at the baby, Lance felt every bit as proud as he was for saving XRZ29B from destruction.

The men at the control tower had also collected their composure and returned to their stations. When Lance returned, they and Surealia were quick to acknowledge that, had not Lance taken command, they would have all been doomed. One person who declined to show appreciation, however, was Stellar Odin, who seethed indignantly for having been ousted from his post.

"I had control of this ship!" Stellar insisted. "And I was just about to get her leveled off!" he blurted, as he brushed himself off from the ordeal. Lance grabbed Stellar by his collar. Looking into the young man's red-flushed face, he suddenly realized the young pilot had done the best he could under the circumstances, and he loosened his grip. Lance knew that even a seasoned pilot could crumble under the same pressure. Lance also saw something in Stellar's face that reminded him of himself, when he'd been a young, brash pilot. For a few moments he envisioned himself as he was back then. Then he turned his much needed attention back to the present moment.

"Who is captain on this shift?" he demanded, eyeing around the room for a response. "Why was Stellar left in control?"

The men were reluctant to answer. They were well aware who the captain in charge was, but they also knew that he was not a person to reckon with. They looked at one another, not wanting to be disobedient to Lance; neither did they want to be on bad terms with the missing captain who had shirked his duty.

Surealia daringly spoke up. "Marcus Marson was scheduled to be on duty, sir!" She was more eager to have Captain Lance Locke be aware of her charms than to be afraid of Captain Marson. Surealia moved closer to Lance, in fact, a little closer than necessary. She looked up at him admiringly, with her wide slanted eyes surrounded with fake, long dark eyelashes. It was obvious to the other men that she was smitten by the handsome captain. "Captain Marcus Marson handed the controls over to Stellar," she boldly announced. "Some of us questioned his orders, but he threatened to demote us or even remove us from our positions if we objected." Surealia hoped Lance would welcome her attention as much as her information. Lance, however, was unaffected by her charming wiles; he was already in love and firmly dedicated to Celestia, his soon-to-be bride. Realizing she was getting nowhere with Lance, Surealia lifted her head with her nose in the air as she made her way back to her post. She knew the other men were making fun of her for making up to Lance.

Lance searched the faces of the crew, and then demanded, "Well, where is Captain Marson? Why would he leave his post at a time like this?"

"I . . . I don't know, Sir," Stellar answered. He sheepishly softened his indignation when he realized he was not going to be held responsible for the ship's plight. "He left and turned the controls over to me just before everything started going haywire. He said he had something to check out. He told me he would be back in a few minutes." Stellar looked up at Lance apologetically and added, "But he never came back!"

Lance was becoming quite suspicious regarding Captain Marson's actions. He wondered why Marson would put a young inexperienced pilot in such a strategic position in lieu of one of the more knowledgeable crew now on duty.

"Well, find him!" Lance exclaimed. The other three crewmen ran off to find the missing captain.

It wasn't long before word came back, via the intercom, from one of the men in the search party. "Captain Locke . . . Marson's shuttle rocket ship is gone!"

Lance fumed. "Apparently our friend Captain Marson was checking something out all right! That something was himself!"

CHAPTER 2

EARTH

Lights flashed across the evening sky as shuttle ships ferried the Hybridites to space stations, which hovered silently beyond earth's fragile atmosphere.

The Hybridites believed, as legend and fact, that war rampaged across the earth; when the present ruling class came into power, war ceased. No one could remember the happy day when that came about or the circumstances that led up to that reviled destruction. Perhaps the shock of a huge nuclear war had brought people to their senses, or maybe a gradual dawning of a higher intelligence was the motivating force. Whatever the catalyst, a defensive arsenal had been manufactured for implementation in the event that an unfriendly civilization might decide to invade the earth.

History before the Honorable Order Of The Source dictated by the Hybridite's ruler, Zarno, had been long forgotten. Nevertheless, writers who hoped to become wealthy or famous from their theories wrote many books in speculation of the subject. How was one to know the truth of the matter? All signs or evidence regarding the past had either been deeply buried due to war or natural disasters; or deliberately excluded from education over the centuries. Besides, the Hybridites thought, what difference would it make now? After all, they had to cooperate and stick together for the purpose of what the president and ruling officers called the Cause. They were convinced the earth had to be evacuated and time was running out. Not only was the population getting out of control, but, according to high government officials, psychics had predicted that in the near future earth would be a useless cinder floating in space. It would be a dim reminder of the way life once was on the beautiful blue planet near the edge of the Milky Way.

Lance's fiancée, Celestia Stevens, had been working more hours for the Cause than should have been expected of anyone. Night came and went too quickly for Celestia. She could only remember lights of space ships going back and forth before falling asleep; it seemed daylight arrived too soon to prod her sleepy eyes to a squint. Adjusting to the brightness, she lazily climbed out of bed, grabbed her silvery silk bathrobe and slipped into it. She stretched as she approached the window of her 200-story penthouse apartment window. As was her habit, she gazed through a telescope to watch the scene below. Hundreds of bubble-like translucent biospheres reflected the morning sunlight, giving the effect of ocean waves. Celestia's mind wandered as she contemplated her future. She imagined really being by the ocean. As she continued to look through the telescope, she thought about her future wedding plans with Lance Locke. Celestia could hardly wait to get married. She wanted to spend their honeymoon on a space cruise, but decided to go to the ocean since Lance had to spend so much time in space as it was. They had agreed on a ten-year marriage contract, with the right of renewal. Surely they would want to renew; Celestia was certain of that. After all, she and

Lance were perfect for each other, so how could it be otherwise? After being married for a while they could create their children. It would be so much fun choosing their children's looks and attributes. It was so easy for Hybridites to have children. After all, there was no painful childbirth as with the Barbarian mothers. All they had to do was agree on the details. It was no wonder the Hybridites were overpopulating. A pang of guilt swept over Celestia, knowing more children were not recommended. She couldn't do anything about it, that's just the way it was she reasoned.

Continuing to look out the window, Celestia noticed some of the Barbarian workers arriving to work in the biospheres. From her viewpoint they looked like ants crawling to work, later to return home to their dreary lives, with no hope of a better future. She felt sorry for them. The Hybridites considered the Barbarians the highest of the animals and were puzzled as to how they could speak when the other animals couldn't. Although they were not regarded as equals, the Barbarians were usually treated with compassion. In general they were approached kindly, but with strict discipline, like one would treat a pet. Many Hybridites even donated their cast off clothing, and other harmless objects that had been legalized for the Barbarians' use, which was a concession made by the government in order to appease the public. Although the clothing was too small, the material was diligently and often imaginatively pieced together by the Barbarians to fit.

Celestia's trance was suddenly broken as she remembered her promise to show up for work . . . even though it was supposed to be her day off. With a sigh, she began her usual morning routine. It was harder than usual with Lance being away . . . just work, work, work, and another evening alone, but dutifully she gathered up the fortitude needed for the tasks ahead. Celestia didn't feel like talking to Roberta, her roboputer, which was created to look and act like a maid, so she merely pointed to commands for her choice of clothes and the date.

A loud buzz startled Celestia, as Roberta announced, "Error, error, your work clothes should be white."

Celestia shouted back, "I don't want to wear my white uniform today; this is my day off and I'm going to wear what I want!"

Red lights in Roberta's eyes lit up, but, as if being embarrassed by the chastisement, she hurriedly complied with Celestia's wishes. From a door in the wall that looked like a closet, a complete set of clothes, tidily hanging on a hanger, emerged. Celestia dropped her silvery robe, kicked off the matching silver slippers and slithered into the iridescent peacock blue and green outfit. Roberta, who had assembled various options that would be most complimentary for Celestia, had designed the clothes. The directions were sent to the manufacturer where the order was filled, then sent directly to Celestia's closet to be summoned at will.

Celestia was pleased with her flattering clothes. She went to the kitchen, then poured and gulped down an energizing breakfast of green liquid. She swallowed a pill which kept her hair blonde, the shade of many Barbarians. Her hair was naturally red. Going blonde was a fad that had caught on with the more fashionable Hybridites.

Celestia grabbed her essentials belt and quickly clipped it around her slender waist. As she raised her hand toward a door, it opened and a tube-like entrance appeared. Once she was safely in the tube, it gradually tilted until she was in a lying-down position on the padded surface of the cubicle. She announced her destination and the tube zoomed to another part of the massive 'Live and Work' complex. Arriving at its destination, the tube realigned itself to an upright position and opened. Celestia stepped out into a room of sterile steel and whiteness.

"Well, whad'cha think of the news?" a slightly preoccupied voice queried, breaking the quietness of the morning. The white-haired man seated at the lab table did not look up from his work as he spoke.

"What news?" asked Celestia.

"Lance!"

"What about Lance?" Celestia probed.

The old man finally raised his head to look at her. He wore a disapproving expression of incredulity. "You mean to tell me you've been so busy with your marriage plans you don't even know what's going on?"

"I haven't had time to listen to the news," explained Celestia. She tightened her lips and hunched her shoulders. Her eyes rolled up, betraying her attempt to hide her impatience. "What's going on with Lance now?"

"Oh, nothing wrong, nothing wrong," the old scientist mumbled, raising his hand in a waving motion as if to erase any misunderstanding. "It's just that he's to be cited for a heroic accomplishment to be awarded at the Capitol at California Island." The scientist tried to act unconcerned. He turned away from Celestia, increasing her curiosity.

Her eyes widened as her gaze returned from the ceiling and her shoulders resumed a normal position. "An award? California Island? What for? When?"

"Well, here . . . here's the article . . . read it for yourself," said the white-haired man nonchalantly. He handed her a newsletter then turned back to his project.

"Isn't it wonderful? I love California Island . . . why just this morning I was thinking about the ocean, and I've got all the right outfits designed   stored in my roboputer for just the right occasion!" Celestia rambled on in her excitement. "And we'll . . ." Dr. Hall didn't let her finish speaking.

"What makes you think you're going?" the old man gruffly interrupted, "We've got work to do right here! Don't you know we've got important work to do for the Cause?"

Celestia dropped her head. Her face became long. As she obediently carried a tray of crawling insects to her lab station, she wore the expression of a reprimanded child. She failed to see a smirk beginning at the corner of the professor's mouth as she began to pout. She mumbled under her breath reasons why she should be able to join Lance and share his big moment. She glanced at the professor out of the corner of her eye, and caught his broadening smile.

"Why you old fossil!" she exclaimed. "You knew all the time it would be okay for me to go to California Island!" Her spirits raised, Celestia went back to sorting a tray of insects. Now she was on good terms with the professor. She thought about how he had discovered cloning beetles to save crops. She remembered that if it weren't for his idea, half the population would have starved; insecticides had killed off most of the helpful insects that kept nature in precarious balance. Celestia felt good about working with the professor. Continuing her work, she put one group of beetles in a screen covered tray, and the non-useful ones into a vat of liquid, which quickly dissolved them. The keepers were put into a freezing unit to later be thawed for use in the biospheres, as needed. The process, while not her favorite, was continued until a quota was filled, and at that point she could resume more interesting other duties.

"We'll need to breed more insects for use in the future – just in case there aren't any on another planet!" she blurted.

The professor turned toward Celestia. "*If* there is a livable planet out there," he retorted in a serious, slightly sad tone.

"Surely we'll find another," said Celestia. She was still in too happy a frame of mind to be daunted. "Just imagine how immense the universe is," she added . . . "You know there would have to be lots of planets fit for us to live on."

"Well, we tried the moon and found it only good for mining, and Mars once had a civilization but isn't able to support life anymore." The professor went on, explaining the slim prospects of life on other planets. "Our only hope is to further explore space, and no one has been able to do that yet. Time, according to the latest news from the Source, is running out" he added despondently. "In the meantime we'll just have to keep shuttling people out to space stations and hope to God there'll be an answer for our people!"

"God . . . God! Did I hear you say God? Why Professor Hall, I didn't know you believed in God! Are you serious? Do you really believe in all those old mythological tales?" Celestia was puzzled.

"I have heard something that makes me wonder. You know, Celestia, ever since our people acquired the wisdom of the Source, perhaps 2,000 years ago or maybe even more, some say that's when the belief in a supreme being called God was abolished. I know things must be better since. . . or so it seems. . . but for some reason I just have this feeling that, well. . . there was more to those old religious beliefs than we admit. . . or that the leaders who receive information from the Source don't want us to know about."

This was the first time Celestia had heard Professor Hall talk openly about the possibility that Zarno and the other leaders might be withholding information from the people. "Professor!" she exclaimed. "I hope you don't go around telling anyone else how you feel. You'll be put in prison . . . or worse yet." Celestia didn't want to speculate any further about the potentially dire consequences. "Besides, our president and leaders at California Island would know if there was anything to those old tales and they only mean well for us. Even our prominent scientists agree with our leaders."

"Not all of the scientists," Dr. Hall mumbled quietly under his breath, in order to avoid a confrontation with Celestia as he turned once more to his work.

Because of the danger of losing his position, the professor would never publicly acknowledge his feelings, and also for the immediate need of the people. Seeing the professor's concern she tried to console him. "Anyway, we'll find an answer," she assured him. Quietly the two dedicated scientists resumed their work. Celestia didn't mind working now that she could look forward to the trip to California Island with Lance.

CHAPTER 3

THE CAPITOL

Celestia and Lance were enjoying the pomp and circumstance of California Island, unaware that Alex Taylor was making a discovery in Egyptralia, and making plans to leave for Jameripan.

"California Island! It's amazing!" Lance commented as he, Celestia and the crew of XRZ29B disembarked from the HOOTS official hovercraft.

"Amazing? Why is it so amazing?" Celestia questioned.

"Well, just think . . . a couple of days ago I was out in space thinking I might not be around another day, and here we are getting the red carpet treatment from the president!"

A loud din was heard as masses of Hybridites were chanting HOOTS over and over while waving flags and shaking noisemakers in honor of Lance and his crew. Officers had to hold back the cheering crowd when a platform lowered the celebrated arrivals from the hovercraft. The media pressed as close as possible for the coveted news. Celestia was glad her wardrobe was in order for the upcoming marriage ceremony. She decided to bring it for this special occasion, hoping she and Lance could get married while they were in the capitol city. Celestia happily smiled and posed for the cameras while Lance, a man of few words, simply nodded at the crowd and modestly gave recognition to his crew. To Lance's relief, they were soon hurried away from the commotion. Once removed from the hubbub of the crowds, Lance felt much more at ease. Lance and Celestia were escorted to the hotel lobby where they could get keys to their rooms.

The clerk at the front desk was obviously used to dealing with the rich and famous. With nose in the air and an affected manner, he did not look up when he asked, "Names please?" Lance responded with both names.

"Yes, I have two rooms, one for you, and one for a Miss Celestia Stevens, both in your name Mr. Lech." Not bothering to look up, the clerk snobbishly told Lance, and then Celestia, to look into the eye activator to program their hotel room doors with their individual retinas.

"That's Locke, Captain Lance L. Locke!" Lance irritatingly emphasized.

The hotel clerk looked up, horrified at his blunder. "Oh, Captain Locke, yes of course, I am so-o-o sorry!"

"Come on, Celestia!" Lance fumed. Miffed, Lance grabbed her arm while she tried to muffle a snicker at the misunderstanding of the clerk.

Since it was still early in the day, Lance and Celestia went for a walk around the manicured grounds. California Island, being the HOOTS capitol, was richly cared for. Gardens and fountains, with every kind of amenity graced the island. Money, it seemed, was no object here.

Having calmed down after the insult by the hotel clerk, Lance felt unusually playful. He picked Celestia up and swung her around. "Isn't it great? Ahhh, this is the life! No more space city, at least for a while. Good ol' green grass, trees, mother earth, and oh yeah . . . you!" he emphasized with an afterthought to tease Celestia. Lance gently lowered her to the ground. He took a deep breath, as if to store up the beauty of their surroundings along with the fresh flower-scented air.

"Let's find our rooms before getting some lunch," Lance suggested in the late morning. As they were searching the hall for their rooms, he tried to ignore Celestia's teasing comments about the earlier confrontation with the clerk. "Hey, room 2050. Now that was a good year, the year of the transition from an old civilization to the new, or so the Barbarians say. Do you think they gave me this room on purpose?"

"Now why would they do that do you suppose?" Celestia looked up at Lance innocently, as if they didn't know. Lance didn't say anything, but being a faithful and true believer in the Cause, he proudly radiated the honor bestowed upon him.

Entering the hotel room, Celestia gasped in admiration at the lavish furnishings. "Wow! Can you believe this?" The words were hardly out of her mouth when Lance picked her up and threw her on the perfectly made bed and tickled her for laughing at him.

"Now look what you've done. We've just arrived and you've already begun messing up the place!" The two continued the teasing, wrestling like children until Celestia, breathlessly, wailed for mercy. She was no match for Lance.

"Look!" she suddenly cried, tilting her head toward the window. Momentarily, fooled by this old trick, Lance loosened his grip as he stretched to look out the window. Celestia grabbed her chance, slipped out of his grasp and ran laughing through the connecting doorway to her own room. She was so impressed by the lavish decorations, she let down her guard and ran back to tell Lance to come look at her room. "Isn't it beautiful?" Celestia opened the door to show Lance, who like her, seemed to be through with acting silly. It was a surprising mistake as Lance embraced her again.

"Well, well, well, what do you know? Here's another bed. Let's see if we can mess this one up too!"

"No, no, Lance!" Celestia began to lose her footing as she attempted to keep him from dragging her toward the bed. Suddenly, in an about face manner, Lance looked at his watch and starkly announced, "Time to go to lunch!" He loosened his grip and let Celestia slip all the way to the floor in a sudden heap as he headed toward the hallway.

Celestia's large, gold, almond shaped eyes narrowed to a squint of determination as she pulled a pillow from the bed and threw it across the room at him.

With that, Lance ran back to Celestia as if to continue their mock battle, but instead he lifted her to her feet. Pulling her closer to him he locked his eyes on hers. Both of their eyes, in Hybridite fashion, glowed in different colors acknowledging their mutual love for each other. Celestia found herself, once again, caught off guard. She quickly closed off her mind so that Lance's advances could not continue. Although gravely disappointed, yet being a gentleman, Lance temporarily drew back. He knew that Celestia was fully resigned on waiting for such intimacy until they signed their marriage contract. Lance, however, was not to be turned away altogether. He pulled Celestia close and passionately pressed his wanting lips against hers. As Lance once again headed for the door, Celestia's eyes flashed in glowing colors of love; more in complete surprise than passion, for it was a very unordinary and unexpected gesture indeed, for a Hybridite!

CHAPTER 4

CELEBRATION

On the day of the celebration, Hybridites jammed the city of California Island to watch the parade in honor of Captain Lance L. Locke and his crew. Colorful floats of every description made their way through the streets lined with spectators yelling HOOTS in honor of the president and the Source; they cheered for the spectacle that passed before their eyes. There were floats laden with flowers designed like recent and past inventions of their race. Politicians and celebrities waved ceremoniously to the crowd, and were greeted back with cheers. There were many marching bands with gloriously designed banners. Instead of soldiers, rows and rows of security police passed down the parade route. The Hybridites had been told that the security police were there for their protection, a ruse provided so as to provide protection in case of any possible outside problems, like an uprising of the Barbarians (which of course, they would never be able to accomplish under the circumstances of their situation). The entire city was alive with excitement and celebration. The president and his staff appeared before the populace receiving, what was to them, their due cheers and reverence. The poor duped Hybridites were totally unaware of the fate that loomed before them as they continued their wildly enthusiastic revelry.

After some time, Lance and Celestia were worn by the energy and excitement of the event. They were famished and returned to their rooms to freshen up before moving on to their next event, a luncheon fit for their celebrity status. They gorged themselves on the sautéed insects, algae casserole and other culinary delicacies as they chatted with other invited guests.

The remainder of the afternoon was planned as free time for the honorees. They could partake of activities of one's own choosing. They could watch a variety of sporting events or even participate if they chose. They could head off to see the usual tourist sights of the great metropolis, or just amble along the palm-lined shore and enjoy the solitude of the flower-laden gardens. It was up to each to select their own venue for some down time between the scheduled events. The evening hours were reserved for a formal banquet, followed by a program given in Lance's honor. The happy, very much in love couple chose the more restful activity of ambling arm-in-arm and sitting in the gardens, admiring and listening to the splashing water of the fountains. The afternoon went all too quickly and it was too soon time to return to their accommodations to freshen up again. This time, they would be donning their finest clothing for what would surely be an evening full of festivities. Lance and Celestia wanted plenty of time so they could arrive at the auditorium cool, rested and relaxed.

Set at the top of a mountain, Universal Hall glistened like a jewel in the middle of the sparkling blue waters surrounded by well-kept gardens. The facade of the front hall had crystal pillars that shone like rainbows, radiating brilliant colors in every direction. The golden domed buildings architecture resembled a palace. The magnificent structure was framed on either side by silvery buttresses that housed light-beamed elevators rising to the upper stories where the lavish offices of government officials were located. The lower story walls were built of strong, transparent glass-like material that could be opened, and the air inside was controlled to provide comfort to its inhabitants no matter what the weather was outside. An invisible shield around the perimeter kept out insects and birds. Above the great façade of the front entrance to the building was an inscription that read The Honorable Order Of The Source. As Lance and Celestia entered the massive hall they witnessed the finest convention staff ever assembled and saw what the best chefs in the domain had prepared for the ceremony. All of the Hybridite guests who attended the event relished a sumptuous dinner. Amid the babble of the noisy throng, when plates were empty and forks were laid down, the master-of-ceremonies approached a podium in the center of the stage that was lined with owl-embellished flags. The high-ranking officer stood quietly until a hush fell over the crowd. Then with a loud commanding voice he proceeded to announce an introduction. "It is with great pleasure that I can introduce to you the president of the Honorable Order Of The Source, President ZARNO!"

All eyes were keenly fastened on the president. The Hybridites went wild yelling "HOOTS", waving flags and rattling noisemakers. They did not clap, because clapping would not be heard from their long slight hands. To the Hybridites, President Zarno was an imposing figure. He pompously strode to the center of the stage. His uniform was embellished with an owl, the emblem of his office. He gazed steadily at the audience, waiting long enough to gain their rapt attention before speaking. Then his words rang boldly throughout the hall.

"People of the Honorable Order Of The Source! Ever since the knowledge of the Source has become known to our universal brotherhood, we have been greatly blessed. Our forefathers passed down the ability to decode the messages from the Source, and it has been not only a privilege, but also a duty for me and our leaders to guide you, the people of our civilization, in the best way possible. We have lived in peace; we have no enemies. We have prospered by mutual cooperation among the people, stamping out disease, poverty and crime until they are almost non-existent. All of this is due to the supreme guidance of the Source, which I of course, have been able to interpret. We must honor the Source and our ancestors who gave it to us for the good of all people. Our lives have improved and become more prosperous because the Source relieves us of having to make decisions by ourselves. We don't have to dwell on or vacillate between our thoughts of what is right or what is wrong. We are free of such indecision. We are totally free of the burden of thinking! Of course as you realize, we must make daily choices, such as what we will have for dinner, or where we will go for entertainment; also, the usual minor mundane things in life, but not the major decisions that might lead us astray." Zarno waited for the roar of the enthusiastic applause and hoots from the audience to subside, which of course, he relished like some gooey spider-laden candy he had eaten earlier. After a few moments he raised his hands to quiet the crowd, and then he continued with his devious speech.

"It is with great humility and regret, that I must reveal to you this following message. Unfortunately, the Source has sadly predicted that a meteor traveling in our direction will have catastrophic consequences to our planet, and could mean the end of our earth, as we know it." A gasp, followed by a hush, fell upon the crowd. "I can ensure you that we shall not be exterminated . . . and our society will persevere! Thankfully, the Source has also provided me with unfathomable wisdom, which I am able to relay to you tonight. We will continue to earnestly work together for the Cause, and for the safety of our people. However, there are some," he stated sarcastically, "who are not authorized by our government that are spreading rumors. They claim that the earth is not in danger, and they are spreading their terrible lies among our citizens. Well, I do not want to be a doomsday nay-sayer, but we must not be fooled. I tell you, in order to protect our beloved Hybridites; we must continue our work of salvation. We must work to save you, your children and those who are yet to come. We will not give up until every man, woman and child has the opportunity of transferring to a space station and thereby increase the chance of survival for all. We will not despair, for it is likely that after the meteor hits our planet, we will be able to return from the safety of the space stations and resume life on earth once it is inhabitable." As Zarno increased his volume to emphasize their return to earth, the band began playing to rouse a positive response of cheers and hoots from the audience.

With this false hope broadcasted at the end of the president's speech, the crowd went wild with enthusiasm and support. The hoots echoed throughout the hall at a feverish pitch. The souvenir rattles marked with the HOOTS emblem added to the din. Relishing in the response to his speech, President Zarno waited before raising his hands, motioning the crowd to quiet down again. "And now," the president again waited for the still prevalent noise to subside; "And now," he repeated, "now the moment we have all been waiting for! I want to call up to the stage the officer, Captain Lance L. Locke! He demonstrated outstanding heroic action beyond his duty to the Cause while onboard space station XRZ29B. I am raising him to the designation of *Commander* Lance L. Locke!" As Lance approached the stage the crowd hooted and rattled their noisemakers more than ever for their hero. In true Lance Locke fashion he humbly accepted the award and modestly gave the credit to his magnificent crew. Celestia tingled with pride, while Zarno, full of contempt for Lance, tried to hide his true feelings for Lance spoiling his plans to get rid of the overpopulated Hybridites.

With the formalities over, the vast majority of attendees gravitated to the grand ballroom where a band had already started playing music to greet their audience. Zarno's girlfriend, Marsiti, was wandering around flashing her eyes at several of the male Hybridites; they did not dare make advances even though they wanted to. They were well aware that one of Zarno's staff would be watching. Zarno believed that Marsiti was *his* property. After the initial greeting of the guests by the band, Marsiti was summoned to the stage. As she wiggled her way to the microphone, the band signaled an introduction. The crowd hushed in anticipation. Marsiti was dressed in a slinky, shimmering, sequined white gown that enhanced her figure; it sparkled with brilliant colors from the spotlights that beamed down on her. She sang a provocative torch song, more like a Barbarian rather than a Hybridite. The audience stomped and shouted for more. She sang a second song, this time moving her hips and shaking castanets to the music with a South American beat. After Marsiti sang, the band continued to play for others that were brought in to entertain the crowd. The band's first set concluded with a mesmerizing heavy rock tune with flashing lights and confetti as a final tribute to Commander Lance L. Locke.

The evening continued and many were devoted to dancing, when much to Celestia's surprise, she noticed an unlikely guest for such an occasion. She leaned into Lance during the dance and said, "Can you believe it? It's Jane!" The two caught Jane's eye. Jane smiled, nodded to her friends from across the room, and excused herself to her companion.

Jane approached the couple, aware of Celestia's surprise and said sarcastically, "You didn't think a Barbarian like me could crash a party like this, did you?" "Well, it just goes to show, you shouldn't jump to conclusions." True, Barbarians were allowed to socialize somewhat with the Hybridites, and any Barbarians present at this event were only admitted by a special invitation. "See that man over there?" Jane's long, dark hair swirled over her shoulder as she swung her head around in her companion's direction. "That's my friend Leo; he brought me. Of course I told him I was a friend of yours, and so . . . here I am!" She smirked at the two and followed up by saying, "I'd better get back before he disappears on the arm of some other flashy female." Jane's hair swirled again as she turned and began walking toward her companion for the evening. As she glanced back at Lance and Celestia, her swirling hair revealed an uncomplimentary birthmark on her back below her shoulder. Sensitive to the mark; she quickly brushed her hair back to cover it. To divert any attention to her actions, she moved her slender, curvaceous body in an obviously sultry manner toward Leo. The guests at the table next to the dancing couple laughed at Jane's antics as Celestia called to her, "If you're still here tomorrow, join us for breakfast!" Jane turned once more and nodded with a slight salute, in a Lauren Bacall style manner, as she disappeared amidst the crowd of celebrants.

As soon as Jane was out of sight, Lance chided Celestia saying, "Well, we're going to have Plain Jane joining us for breakfast tomorrow morning, hmmm?"

Celestia unwittingly responded, "Oh, Lance, stop calling her that. Jane is so nice, even if she is a Barbarian. Besides, I like her, and she can't help it if she has that funny bulgy figure. Most Barbarian women are built that way. I guess it's their heredity and primitive diet."

Lance toyed with his near empty cup as Celestia went on about Jane. His mind had drifted to thoughts of Jane, not in the scientific way of Celestia's, but rather of Jane's curvy charms. It was as if some invisible thread from the past tugged at him, arousing feelings he had and could not understand. Lance was startled back to reality as Celestia broke his introverted thoughts, "You can stand to sit through one little breakfast with Jane, can't you? Can't you Lance?" Celestia repeated a little louder, trying to get Lance's attention and a response.

Lance fumbled with his cup again, almost dropping it as Celestia's voice pierced his fantasy. Coming out of his dreamlike trance, he once again focused attention on Celestia. Now back to his normal senses, he began to realize how beautiful Celestia really was. He gazed at the light shining through her cottony blonde hair. She looked like some ethereal being, an angel with a halo framing her dainty porcelain-like features. Admiring her beauty, he hesitated to answer, finally responding, "What? Uh, oh, okay, one little meal." Lance feigned disgust in order to tease Celestia, however, at the same time it once again puzzled him as to why he had thought about Jane as he did.

"Lance, remember you have some Barbarian friends, too", Celestia pointed out as she justified the breakfast with Jane.

Lance justified in return, "That's different. Besides, we don't just socialize, we talk about important things . . . come on, Celestia, let's dance!" Lance changed the subject; he pulled her close and onto the dance floor; leaving his mind troubling images of Jane behind him.

Hybridite dancing was unique to say the least. Lance was dressed in white formal attire. Celestia's skin-tight outfit was of iridescent colors surrounded by a sheer material that wafted with each movement, shining with rainbow-like colors, reminiscent of a spider web in the sun after a rain. The two faced each other stiffly like statues without touching. They stared into each other's eyes. As the music filled the air, they began subtle movements beginning with unique facial expressions. Looking in different directions with slightly jerky movements, they mentally choreographed their dance to which they moved in precise, expertly synchronized steps. At first their moves were stiff and robot-like, but gradually they became more graceful with intricate swirls and even some amazing lifts. They seemed to rise off the floor like luminous butterflies. The room was soon filled with other Hybridites flitting about in their colorful evening attire. As lights flashed intermittently upon them in time to the music from futuristic instruments, they continued dancing well into the night.

CHAPTER 5

AN EVIL PLAN

The day after the celebration, Marcus Marson had to report to Zarno. Hearing that Marcus had arrived and was awaiting an invitation to enter his office, Zarno waved Marsiti off through another door. Before summoning Marcus, he grabbed some insect laden algae candy. Like a naughty schoolboy, he stuffed it in his mouth and quickly devoured it. He wiped his face, but missed some of the candy; a long legged spider clung to the corner of his mouth and chin. The spider escaped being eaten, but was caught in the gooey mess. Marcus was nervously sitting in the waiting room. Finally the secretary broke the silence. "The president will see you now," she coolly stated. Startled, Marcus jumped up, then cautiously approached the president's door. After a moment's hesitation, he gained enough courage to enter. Frightened, he frantically searched for something to say that would soften the anger he knew the president would barrage upon him. Trying to mask his fear, he stood at attention. President Zarno did not turn to face Marcus immediately. Instead, Marcus was given a show of power that Zarno presented by the decor of the office. Scenery lit up the walls like a movie showing scenes of grandeur. Holograms of parades seemed to come right through the walls. Zarno was portrayed as being worshiped by the people as he and his entourage passed by. Another wall was lined with shelves of trophies from honors that had been bestowed upon him.

After Zarno felt that enough of the wonders of his accomplishments had been displayed, he slowly turned toward Marcus. Zarno's attempt to impress Marcus worked. Zarno himself did not only impress Marcus, but the display of his power made him even more fearful of him. While still standing at attention, Marcus tried to cover his surprise as he noticed the spider hanging on the candy that drooled down Zarno's chin. The live spider wiggled as it dangled by one leg from the gooey mess.

"You fool!" Zarno blurted. "I gave you every opportunity to be successful in your assignment!" He again shouted while sitting behind his huge desk in front of the window. Even more shocking than the drooled candy, president Zarno's desk rose above the frightened Marcus Marson as if by magic. Looking down on him, Zarno continued. "You had full cooperation from my staff!" The scene would have been laughable if Zarno's show of power had not broken down Marcus' attempt to be unnerved. He was almost frozen with fear. He dared not laugh at the sight of the spider struggling to get loose from the candy. Marcus could see the similarity of his own predicament for he desperately wanted to get loose from Zarno's fury.

"But . . . but . . . Mr. President," Marcus pleaded, "you saw what happened through your crystal scope and I almost didn't have time to escape!"

Thunder rumbled in unison with the angry president's sharp rebuke. Bright flashes of lightening revealed raindrops slithering in snake-like rivulets down the large window behind him. "Don't tell *me* what I saw!" Zarno leaned forward over his desk even more as he shouted, shaking his fist. "I know what I saw, I saw Failure!" The excessively large Hybridite's puffy face reddened as the slobbers of candy drooled even more as he angrily spurted out obscenities. The force of his shouting freed the spider to fall down on Marcus. As Marcus followed the spider's path with his eyes, Zarno yelled, "You were supposed to steer station XRZ29B straight for a black hole before getting out of there. You left your station to some young punk and jumped in your rocket ship much too soon. Did you have second thoughts and change direction?" Zarno looked slyly at the captain trying to trick him into a confession. Being suspicious of him as with everyone else, he continued his accusations. Then he slunk back in the darkness of his big chair, folded his hands and deviously changed the tone of his voice to a cooing plea. "Now, Captain Marson, I know it seems harsh. I've been suffering from feeling sorry for all of those people on the station myself." Feigning sympathy, he continued. "But you . . . you understand, don't you, that the raw truth of the matter is we just cannot save all of the people. Now we can't let them know that, can we? The population is getting out of hand. We don't want a massacre on our hands, or war, or to have thousands of Hybridites dying a slow cruel death, do we? Believe me, it's for the best. Why the whole population would panic if they knew the truth. No, you've got to get hold of yourself and you know how important you are to me and my staff. We have given you confidential information from the Source for the good of the Cause. You can see it our way now, can't you? And we can depend on you in the future, can't we?" The smooth talking president fed his words to the gullible Marcus putting him on the spot. Captain Marcus Marson had no alternative. He had to agree.

"Yes Sir! You can depend on me for the good of the people," the captain responded with a salute.

Zarno waited a few moments after Marson left before he snapped orders over the invisible voice-wave emitter to his secretary. "Get my staff over here for a meeting," he ordered, "I want them here now!"

Before his staff arrived, Zarno lowered his desk. Marsiti had come back. While buttering up to Zarno, she teased him about getting into the candy. "Now Zarno, baby. You mustn't eat so much candy." Zarno looked up at Marsiti sheepishly enjoying her doting attention. She had just enough time to wipe more of the insect laden candy from his mouth and chin before the entering staff was announced. After Zarno waved the giggling Marsiti off a second time, his attitude changed abruptly. He paced back and forth with his arms behind his back. "We're going to have to step up the program, gentlemen; we've got to get rid of as many space stations as quickly as possible without letting the public know what's going on. I'm afraid that . . . that so and so, Lance Locke, is going to catch on to our plans. He's bound to wonder why Marson let that station get so close to a black hole in the first place. Now we can't take any more chances like that. We'll have to be more careful in the future. I have an idea to get him off our backs. It's time, gentlemen, to send our 'hero' on a mission. We're going to send our illustrious friend out to scout for another planet. That, my dear cohorts, should keep him busy and out of our hair for quite some time! When we get the population numbers down far enough, we'll have complete control without any interference. People are beginning to ask too many questions and we can't have that. In the future, the Barbarians will no longer get paid for working in the biospheres; they'll work for nothing and no one will dare resist!" Zarno laughed with a spine tingling laugh as he added, "Those stupid Barbarians aren't good for anything else anyway." Then he smugly announced, "Not only that, but if Locke does find another planet, so much the better! We'll have another world at our disposal. On the other hand, if he doesn't, well then . . ." Zarno's words trailed off as he shrugged his shoulders and puffed out his chest in admiration of himself. He plopped some more wiggling spider candy in his mouth, while leaving his officers to their own inescapable conclusions.

"Sheer inspiration Mr. President that sounds great!" one of the staff members agreed, feeding the tyrant's ego even more in spite of their apprehensions. "We'll put your plan into operation right away." The other staffers nodded in agreement hoping for a crumb of approval from their heartless leader. Instead, Zarno's only response was an abrupt ending of the meeting with a curt, "Good day, Gentlemen!" He quickly turned his back on them. As he looked out the window, lightning flashed, etching grisly patterns across the sky. The men meekly filed out of the office; they shrugged their shoulders and looked at each other dejectedly. They were fully aware of the gruesome task that lay ahead of them, and they knew of only two alternatives. The grim choices were to save themselves or the space stations. That meant one choice or the other, for either Lance, or us, it was . . . Elimination!

CHAPTER 6

INTERLUNERLUDE

The excitement of the ceremony at California Island had subsided. Ripples of sea foam washed over the feet of Lance and Celestia as they lie on the beach. The remainder of their bodies shone with the sliver of moonlight against a blue-black blend of ocean and sky.

"The time has gone by so fast," Celestia murmured. "Tomorrow its back to the bugs!" she pouted. Then she quickly changed her attitude as she leaned over onto Lance's chest. "Oh, let's not think about anything else. Let's just enjoy what's left of our trip. Everything's been so wonderful and just think!" Celestia turned her face to meet Lance's in order to get his rapt attention. "Soon, we'll have a lifetime together. I mean at least ten years." She laughed, still intent on getting a reaction, but Lance did not join in her playful mood. He was preoccupied. He tried not to show it, but he couldn't keep his thoughts to himself any longer. He injected his own concerns out loud while Celestia's rambling continued without fazing him.

Lance also rambled on with thoughts of his own. "That problem on the space station; something just didn't seem right, and that captain, why did he leave his post putting that young pilot in his place? That was a foolish thing to do. It didn't make sense leaving that much responsibility to an inexperienced young crewmember! Why would he leave the station anyway, especially when things weren't going well?" Something was amiss, he thought.

Celestia was in no mood to talk about a space station. "Oh Lance, he probably thought it was in good hands and just left a few minutes early. Maybe he thought it would give the young pilot a chance to get some experience, not realizing there was any danger. After all, he knew it was almost time for your shift to begin and thought it wouldn't be long until you'd be there to take over. Anyway . . . hey! Are you always going to be thinking about such things when you're off duty?"

"I guess not." Lance turned his attention back to Celestia, taking her by the hand. "You're right, let's get a drink at the beach bar before heading back to the hotel." One drink became two, and then a third. The intoxicating beverages had been perfected and soon provided the woozy effect of the liquor. Their thirst for the exotic pungent flavor, the noisy crowd and the beat of funky music lured them on longer than they had intended. As the evening waned the couple waddled dizzily back to their suites trying to muffle their giggles and shushing each other, trying not to draw any attention. They did not want the nosey media people who were in constant search of gossip to find them. Hiding their faces, Lance made several futile attempts to open his room first, since he was the worst for wear. Lance could not hold his eyes open or stand still long enough to get an eye to connect with the hotel door retina scanner. The more he wavered back and forth, the more the couple bent over with laughter. Several disgruntled neighbors peered out their slightly opened doors to see what the disturbance was at such a late hour. Several slammed their doors shut in disgust. When Lance finally succeeded in scanning his retina, the inebriated couple stumbled into his room. As Lance floundered toward his bed, he grabbed Celestia and tried to kiss her. He missed his mark; undeterred, he lunged toward her again.

"Stop Lance, you're acting like a Barbarian!" Still a bit woozy, Celestia giggled as she slipped out of his arms and slurred, "I'll tell you what, you lie here and I'll go to my room and maybe we'll read minds!" Celestia was aware enough to humor Lance even though she had no such intention, for she was determined to wait until their ten-year marriage contract was signed and sealed. She was quite sure that in Lance's condition he was sure to fall asleep before he even had a chance to think.

Lance mumbled as he fell on the bed with his eyes already closed. "Reeaally? You meeaan it?"

"Of course, we'll read minds," Celestia soothed. Being careful to ensure that Lance was safely drifting off to sleep, her words gradually diminished as she tiptoed out of his room. In her own bed, Celestia snuggled up to her pillow. She was restless; and couldn't sleep. Those drinks should have made me drowsy, she thought. Her eyes widened as she realized that Lance wasn't sound asleep after all. In fact, he was trying to probe her mind. "No!" She tried to bar the door of her mind from his advances, but as he persisted probing her mind, she began to give in. "Oh, Lance!" She felt the power of his thoughts. Even though he was in a different room, in a different bed, it felt as if he were there lying up close to her. Celestia's resistance was weakening. Her body trembled slightly as his mental lovemaking was beginning to take over her senses. With intense determination to wait until they were married, Celestia stiffened and closed herself off from his advances. She had won out. Regaining her composure and realizing what had just happened, the color of her eyes began changing rapidly, flashing through all the colors of the rainbow.

Suddenly, her large almond eyes turned bright red, livid with anger because he was able to get that far with her. In the other room, Lance became aware of her frustration and disappointingly sunk back into an inebriated slumber.

Sleep absolved Celestia's anger. Waking to the morning light that was softened by sheer curtains swaying in the breeze of an open window, she stretched. She curled up like a cat and mused on the memories of last night's frolic. She was in awe of her unexpected feeling of well-being, in spite of a tinge of guilt after her close call of succumbing to Lance's desire. Celestia's scientific inclinations took over as she mused about the facts of life. Even though the Hybridite's reproductive organs had become useless after many centuries of non-use, she was amazed at the all-enveloping feeling of love she had experienced. The Hybridite's ancestors preferred having children outside of their bodies and had developed the technology for this a long time ago. They found they could extract the necessary components for creating life from each partner to be used at will when they wanted to reproduce. They could creatively select the specific genes they desired, choosing the exact makeup of their offspring. They had discovered that they could still experience pleasure by opening their minds to each other. In her innocence, Celestia had no idea how wonderful mental lovemaking could be. The warmth of their affection enfolded her as she snuggled more closely to her pillow. Nestled under the silken covers, pervaded by thoughts of Lance, she drifted off into a sea of contentment.

It was still early in the morning when, in another room, Lance was not so relaxed or content. This time it was not because of Celestia, or their unfulfilled lovemaking. Instead, his thoughts again turned inevitably toward space station XRZ29B. He tried to fit the pieces of the puzzle together regarding the quick exit of Captain Marcus

Marson. Maybe I was wrong. Surely I judged him too quickly. Maybe Celestia was right after all, he rationalized. Convincing himself it was all just a mistake, he rolled over and tried to recall the details of that situation until sleep finally forced itself upon him.

CHAPTER 7

AN UNEXPECTED MEETING

There was a knock at Lance's door as a voice echoed down the corridor. "Last call for breakfast! Last call for breakfast!" Lance rubbed his eyes open and winced at the sunlight streaming through the window. He didn't want to miss breakfast, so he reluctantly threw the covers back and swung his legs over the side of the bed. Stretching, he noticed a reflection of someone still lying under the covers. He could hardly believe it. It was Celestia. She must have crept into his bed after he had fallen back to sleep. "It's morning" he gently whispered as he nudged Celestia's unresponsive body. He felt smugly proud of his previous night's endeavors knowing his power of concentration was still intact. He thought that she must have relented regarding her former reluctance to love making. He soon realized that he was sorely mistaken.

"I don't care!" Celestia mumbled from her still motionless body. Determined not to open her eyes she drowsily insisted, "You go on; I don't want any breakfast."

Lance shrugged in disappointment. He thought to himself, at least she wanted to be near him. He smiled to himself and let Celestia slip back into a deep sleep. He showered in a beam of golden light that surrounded his slim yet sturdy physique. Water was used only sparingly on the tender Hybridite skin. Bathed and invigorated by the warm cleansing light, Lance dressed and quietly closed the door, leaving Celestia to her desired slumber. Upon reaching the dining room doorway, Lance hesitated. As his gaze searched for an empty table, a familiar voice beckoned to him.

"Lance, Lance, over here!" The voice belonged to Alex Carter Taylor, one of the few Barbarians Lance had befriended. By a stroke of fate, Alex had just met the beautiful Barbarian, Jane. Their meeting was almost inevitable since there were very few Barbarians present and most of the tables were already taken. Both had entered the dining hall earlier and looked around for a table. Simultaneously, Alex and Jane spotted an empty one and hurried to grab it. Both feeling quite miffed at first, they finally called a truce and shared the table. They hardly had time for introductions when Lance approached. Lance earnestly began questioning Alex.

"What brings you here to California Island, you old renegade? How'd you manage to get a table in this crowd?" Lance taunted Alex as he looked around the room emphasizing the good fortune his friend had in capturing a table, as well as the attention of Jane. "Or did you mooch yourself in with this lovely young lady?" he quipped, nodding in Jane's direction.

"Here, here," Alex protested, "let's not give anyone a bad impression," he jeered at Lance while smiling at Jane. He then continued, "What am I doing here? Why . . . I wouldn't miss your award ceremony for anything. Now, tell me the truth old buddy, who'd you pay off for all this hero hoopla, and how much did it cost you?"

Lance put his hand beside his mouth and leaned over whispering to Jane while making sure Alex could hear. "Don't believe anything this guy tells you. He'll say anything to make an impression on you; but between you and me, he's just blowing smoke." The jab was more than it sounded on the surface, for most Hybridites loathed smoking, a habit that was relished by many Barbarians. Alex pretended to be disgruntled at Lance's comments, but a sheepish grin broke through, betraying his real feelings. It was obvious they were both enjoying some mutual sarcastic buffeting.

Jane interrupted. "Isn't it funny, Alex? I understand you're an archeologist and enjoy digging in the earth." Before Alex could respond, Jane turned to Lance, "And I hear you command a space station. So, I guess we could say you dig in the sky. I'll bet you two have plenty of tales to tell . . . and I promise not to believe a word either of you have to say!" Lance and Alex chuckled. Jane then questioned the whereabouts of Celestia, reasoning sarcastically to the gentlemen, "After all, I don't know if I can manage two liars all by myself."

The waiter had been standing by patiently before finally speaking up, "May I take your order?" Lance was not ready for food yet, but sufficed temporarily to order a revitalizing juice, while Alex and Jane ordered the sparse offerings on the menu for Barbarian guests. Choices made, the two men were eager to catch up on what news each had to tell since their last meeting. Jane listened intently to their adventures, trying to distinguish between fact and fable. Regardless, it was easy to see she was especially interested in Alex no matter what he had to say.

The spell Alex had over Jane was temporarily broken as Celestia finally approached the doorway of the dining hall. Celestia was known to be beautiful; however, standing in the doorway while searching for Lance, she looked exceptionally lovely. It was no wonder that many heads turned toward her. Some of the women admired

Celestia's beauty and some lowered their eyes as if feeling i̇
in her presence. She, obviously or not so obviously, encha
men. Upon spotting Lance, Celestia seemed to float in her ₌ight
beaded, sheer black gown as she glided gracefully over to the table.
Introductions were made, and Lance ordered an extravagant soy and
algae-based meal, with a side of caterpillar soufflé, all complements
of the government in Lance's behalf.

After some light-hearted conversation and a partially consumed breakfast, Celestia excused herself, smiling. "We girls have
more important things to do than sit around and tell tall tales. Come
Jane; let's have some adventures of our own. There's a new shop I
want you to see." Celestia grinned and Jane shrugged her shoulders
in compliance as she looked back at Alex. She was reluctant to leave,
thinking she might not get another opportunity to see him again.

"Don't worry Jane," Celestia whispered, noticing Jane's obvious
interest in Alex. "We'll see them again." Assured by Celestia's confidence, the two girls continued on their way to the elite shopping
area.

As Celestia and Jane vanished out of sight, Alex took on a
more somber mood. "Lance", he began, "my time spent in the remote
areas of archeological digs were not just all fun and games." Alex
looked around to make sure no one else was listening before going
on. "My team and I feel we will make discoveries that will prove the
oral traditions of the 'Old Ones' to be true. They have handed down
information from one generation to another about our history, of
course, which suggests that we come from a higher civilization than
Zarno will allow anyone know about. Our 'Old Ones' tell us of hidden records, probably thousands of years old or more, revealing evidence that the current government, the president and his staff, are
hiding the truth from the people." Alex had tried to be as tactful as

possible attempting to not offend his friend who was especially loyal to Zarno and the officials of the Honorable Order Of The Source. "I came here specifically to warn you, so you might be better prepared when you realize the truth. I doubted the 'Old Ones' too, at first. I thought they were just telling hopeful stories and myths about our history, but now I believe that there is truth in what they have said. I can feel it in my bones!"

"Oh, come on", Lance sneered, "That's preposterous. You don't have any proof. It's just hearsay. Why, our civilization is in the best shape the world has ever known. I think the sun has permeated through your thick skull and melted your brain! You should lay off digging around out there in the desert. You're wasting your time. You Barbarians had better come to your senses and join in our attempts to get secure space stations in outer space, or you'll be left rolling around on a barren spherical cinder one of these days." Lance shook his head back and forth as he looked down at his half empty cup of hot revitalizing liquid. He hoped to convince his friend for his own sake, and for everyone else's, that Alex's fears were unfounded.

Alex ignored Lance's objections and went on trying to persuade him. "Lance, listen to me. You must believe me." Alex lowered his voice again, almost to a whisper, for he knew the penalty for speaking out against the government. "I know what I'm talking about. Those hokies . . ." Alex caught himself as Lance gave him a glaring look; then he continued. "Those guys at the capitol are up to no good. It's true, I don't know exactly what they're up to, but I do know this. They've destroyed records, books, anything they could with regard to historical documentation from when they and their predecessors came into power." Alex again caught himself, this time as his voice rose excitedly. He then lowered his voice once more to a whisper. "Now, I'm not saying that I dislike or distrust all Hybridites .

. . most of you are good hearted, but also misinformed. I tell you, I'm not going to rest until I find out what's going on!"

Lance glanced around to see if anyone was hearing the dangerous words his friend had expounded. "What would be the point?" he questioned.

Alex was getting frustrated. "The point is, my good friend, it is extremely doubtful that the earth is due to be destroyed, and the present powers that be know it!" Alex became emphatic causing Lance to squirm. Alex tried to control his exasperation and continued, once again returning to a low whisper. Somehow he had to convince Lance that he was telling the truth.

Lance looked down at his cup again as if he wasn't listening, but being curious did not interrupt Alex. Soon, Lance became impatient, for he had heard enough of Alex's nonsense. How Alex could be so sure and so brazen to talk to him about our president and our government, he wondered, but he held his temper. "Jane was right." Lance sighed, "You dig in the earth and I'll dig in the sky, and someday one of us will be right." Lance quickly changed the subject in order to avoid an argument. "In the meantime, let's go find out what those two women are up to, before they buy up everything in that new shop." Lance knew Jane wouldn't have enough wages in the form of credit to be able to buy much, if anything. Even though, there would be a small selection of goods for Barbarians. They rarely had the means to buy anything. He also knew, however, that Celestia had a very generous nature.

As the two men turned their attention to searching the shopping area for the girls, Alex couldn't keep from revealing his interest in Jane. "Tell me about Jane. I didn't catch her last name. Where does she live? How did you and Celestia come to know her?"

"You mean Plain Jane?" Lance pretended he was not aware of Alex's interest in her. "No one knows her last name. That's why I call her Plain Jane. Of course that makes Celestia mad, so I don't ever say Plain Jane around her."

"Oh, I wouldn't ever call her that! There's nothing plain about Jane as far as I'm concerned" Alex protested. "Of course, you Hybridites have an entirely different taste in women, I can certainly see that! Any Barbarian would consider Jane a brown eyed, dark haired beauty."

Lance gave a sideways glance at Alex, "Uh…yes, we Hybridites do have a slightly different idea of what's attractive." "Well, I didn't mean that Jane was plain in looks, of course, I just meant we just call her Jane . . . or rather, I call her Plain Jane because she doesn't have a last name. So see? She's just known as Plain Jane to me and some others." It was easy to see Lance was having a difficult time explaining, while Alex simply shook his head in confusion. "Anyway", Lance continued, "Jane is an orphan. At an early age she was found wandering around. No one knows where or who her parents were. Maybe they were so poor they couldn't take care of her. Maybe they hoped someone would take her in and care for her better than they could. No one really knows the truth about the matter, but several Barbarians, who seemed to be doing fairly well, had taken her in for short periods of time, until she was old enough to take care of herself. She never really bonded with anyone in particular though. At one point, Celestia's mother met the Barbarians that Jane was staying with, when she had taken on some volunteer work helping the poor. Celestia's mother took Jane along with her on several occasions during the time that Jane was growing up, so Jane and Celestia often played together. They have remained friends ever since."

Suddenly, Lance came to an abrupt stop. "Say, I think this is the new shop Celestia was talking about. Let's go in and see if we can find the girls." Alex was intrigued by Lance's tale of Jane's past, but he would have to do with what little information he had gotten about her until another time.

After his brief encounter with Lance, Alex returned to Egyptralia, a disappointed man. He was angry with himself for not being able to convince Lance that the oral traditions of the 'Old Ones' held some truth, and he also didn't want his eagerness to cause a rift between them. Alex knew he would need proof, so he wanted to return to the dig as soon as possible. He was also disappointed for not convincing Jane to meet with him on her return. He wondered if he would ever see her again. He was frustrated at the thought of losing her to the man who had taken her to the celebration dinner. No matter what, the most important thing now was to find the proof he needed, and he felt certain and more determined than ever, that he would.

CHAPTER 8

THE MISSION

Lance and Celestia were scheduled to be returning to Jameripan from the ceremonies on California Island. Celestia attempted to find room in her bulging travel bags for her newly purchased souvenirs. She had taken great care in choosing just the right gifts to please her friends at home. A cup bearing the emblem of an owl was stuffed amid her lingerie. She carefully pushed another cup with 'HOOTS' printed on one side, and President Zarno on the other, between some shoes. While she busied herself with the task at hand, Lance received a message from his platinum activator ring, which was engraved in gold with the words, The Honorable Order Of The Source. It was addressed to Commander Lance L. Locke. Preoccupied with her packing, Celestia didn't look up or even pay any attention to what was being said. As Lance ended his call, Celestia fussed, "I can't get everything in my bags. Do you have any extra room in yours?"

"I have something to tell you" Lance answered, ignoring Celestia's plight. "I'm not going back with you."

"Not going back? What do you mean?" Startled by those words, Celestia looked up from her packing in disbelief. "Why not?

Where are you going? I thought you had more time off to spend at home. When are you coming back?" The questions followed one after the other.

"I don't know. It may be a long time. I've got orders. Here, you listen." Lance held his hand out so Celestia could hear the message. She didn't want to hear it.

"Orders? Orders for what?" Celestia put down the cup she was stuffing in her bag and stared at Lance for a moment. Then, as if nothing could stand in the way of their plans, she waved her hand as if to dismiss the message and continued packing. "I don't care what they say, you can just tell them you have time off and you're going to get married."

Lance tried to explain.   "I can't just refuse them, Celestia; I'm going on a mission to outer space . . . beyond the space stations. Farther than anyone has ever gone!" His voice rose as he tried to justify the mission. "It's imperative that we find another planet soon in order to get people off the earth before the disaster strikes. I . . . I'm . . ." Lance was having trouble getting the words out of his mouth, not only because of Celestia's plans were being shattered, but also because of the danger of going into the unknown. He knew what he dared not say; he knew that he might never come back. "I'm going on a scouting mission to find an inhabitable planet." Confused and impatient, he blurted, "It's our only chance of survival, Celestia!" He grabbed the horrified girl, hugging her closely, trying to assure her that everything would be all right, even if he didn't believe it himself.

"Oh Lance," Celestia cried as she pulled away. "You can't go . . . there's no telling how long that will take . . . and who knows if you'll ever come back! Don't do it, Lance, you can turn down the assignment!" Celestia pathetically half ordered and half begged. "Surely, someone else can go instead. You've served enough. Besides, what about our marriage plans? What about us?"

"We'll have to wait, Celestia. It's my duty to go. Don't you see? There are hundreds of space stations with thousands of Hybridites just waiting for a chance of survival. We can't let our personal lives stand in the way!"

"Damn it, Lance!" Celestia shouted through tears; her sorrow turned to anger. "You knew about this all the time we've been here. You knew you had to leave and you deliberately encouraged me to let you read my mind while we were here. If you really loved me you wouldn't go on this insane mission. Well, you just go ahead and go! I'm not signing any marriage contract anyway, not now, not ever. You, you son of a Barbarian!" Celestia yelled louder and with such ferocity that Lance could hardly believe it came out of her. "I don't care if the world does end, or if you ever find another planet. On the other hand, I hope you do find one because this one isn't big enough for both of us!"

"Celestia, I truly didn't know any of this until I got the message just now, and you shouldn't use those Barbarian expressions." Lance tried to calm her down by talking as softly as he could, but she was in no mood to be corrected about her language.

Celestia's eyes flashed with a glow of red and purple neon as she shouted, "Get out. Get out . . . GET . . . OUT!" Furious and frustrated, she raised her arm with one of the newly purchased cups she had in her hand and heftily threw it at him, yelling, "You take this cup and president Zarno with you!" Lance ducked just in time as the flying cup crashed into a mirror behind him. He somehow managed to remain cool and calm when the mirror was shattered to smithereens, like Celestia's plans. Lance knew that trying to reason with her would be useless at this point, so with mixed feelings of duty and guilt, he departed, leaving Celestia sobbing fitfully. It took all of the strength he could muster to keep himself from going back to her. Regaining his composure and returning his thoughts to his sworn duty, he quickly headed toward the post where he was to be briefed in preparation for his mission.

"You'll report back to space station XRZ29B," the cold words rang out indifferently from the officer in charge of the briefing session at headquarters. "You are the most familiar with that station, so that's where you'll receive your training and instructions. This is a secret mission code named, 'Planet Probe'. You will receive all of the expert help and needed supplies during your preparations, and you will be given the utmost regard to ensure your safe return." Lance was completely unaware of the deceit behind the mission, and listened intently to his orders. "We estimate you can exit this solar system with the latest space equipment and technology possible in coordination with an experienced ground crew and personnel. Congratulations on your upgrade to Commander, and also for being chosen for this highly important mission. We will be in close contact at all times regarding your progress Commander Locke. Goodbye and good luck!"

With the briefing over, Lance tried to reach Celestia in hopes he could see her and smooth things over between them before he left. He had hoped that once she got over the shock of his mission she would understand that this was the way it had to be. She did not respond to any of his messages. With a feeling of desperation, he inquired about her at the hotel desk.

"She left about twenty minutes ago." The hotel clerk's words stabbed Lance as he frantically searched the man's face for any glimmer of hope regarding her whereabouts. Finding none, he reluctantly squeezed out a sullen thank you under his breath, leaving the desk

---

clerk still elaborating on Celestia's sudden departure. Lance had no information to go on and he realized that, by now, she could be well on her way back to Jameripan. There was no time to spare. There was nothing left for him to do except get back to making the preparations for the mission ahead.

CHAPTER 9

SCIENCE

While Lance tried to deal with his fate, Celestia also had to deal with hers. When she returned to Jameripan and her career, she felt that everything had been left at loose ends regarding Lance and their future. The excitement and expectations she had at California Island had dwindled down to sheer disappointment. She had to force herself to go back to work. Being conscientious, it was inevitable that she must put duty first.

Celestia hesitated at the door of the laboratory that bore the title DR. NOAH T. HALL. It seemed she had never left at all and she was certainly in no mood to return, especially when it was supposed to be her day off. Her experience at California Island was just like a dream that turned into a nightmare. How different she felt about her career since she and Lance left California Island on such unfriendly terms. She had worked so hard to become a leading scientist, but it all seemed so trivial now. In her heart she knew the reason for her lack of interest. She was still in love with Lance in spite of her rampage. In reflecting on the recent events, she reasoned within herself. Why had she not made amends before they parted? Now it was too late. Lance would be well on his way to who knows where. Would he ever come back from the mission he believed to be necessary?

Celestia also had her share of responsibility. The years of training under the careful scrutiny of Professor Hall raised her position to the crucial point where, if anything happened to him, she would be the only one to carry on his work. It would take too much time to train someone else to the level of her expertise. Celestia was well aware of the importance of her position. Maybe Lance was right; they both must put the welfare of the Hybridites before themselves. Resolved to the fact that she must fulfill her obligation to her people and her government, a prisoner of her own knowledge, Celestia took a deep breath and opened the door.

Things looked different to Celestia since she had been away. Like not seeing the forest for the trees, what she took for granted before now took on a new light. Compassion welled up in her as, for the first time she noticed the frailty of the aging professor. She had been around him so much in recent years she had never noticed. Did it take going away to really see him, she wondered. His back was toward her as she entered the laboratory. He did not immediately turn toward her as she had expected, thinking he would be happy to see her. Instead, the professor slowly peeked around as if hiding something. Finally, turning in full view with a big grin on his face, he revealed a young chimpanzee cradled in his arms.

"Professor Hall, when did you adopt a chimp?" Celestia was startled at first, and then a smile finally appeared on her face, too.

Grinning with the look of the cat that swallowed a canary, Dr. Hall hurried over toward Celestia, greeting her return with his news. "I've done it Celestia, I've made a breakthrough" he exclaimed excitedly.

"What kind of breakthrough? What have you done, Professor Hall?"

"This monkey is not an original, Celestia. It's a duplicate. I cloned it! It not only does it look the same as the original, it has assimilated the same qualities of the original, and it can do tricks that it has never been taught. Just think, if monkeys can be cloned, the next step is . . ." The professor's words dropped off, pausing as his eyes met Celestia's. Her eyes widened with astonishment. Wider than they were naturally, because of the unbelievable information she was hearing when the professor continued, saying, "The next step is cloning Hybridites!"

"Cloning Hybridites!" Celestia gasped. "Professor Hall, why on earth would we want more Hybridites? Have you gone mad? If there's anything we don't need on this planet, it's more Hybridites. Why, we're already working as fast as we can to get the whole race shuttled out to space . . . and off this planet!"

"But this is science, Celestia, don't you see? Science must go on no matter what. Who knows all of the good this knowledge will do for future generations? Look at atomic and nuclear power. Years ago, civilization was almost destroyed, and it was thought atomic and nuclear power could have been the cause; and now look at all the progress we've attained since then because of those discoveries. Now Celestia, don't you worry. This information is just for you and me until further experiments are done. We will tell no one, not even our top officials."

"Experiments? What for? What kind of experiments? It sounds to me you've gotten yourself into a real kettle of fish, or rather a barrel of monkeys I should say."

Dr. Hall rubbed his chin through his sparse white beard. "Well, I still have a few kinks to work out, but they're minor. I'll just have to work on them when I get back." He brushed the problem off as being rather insignificant.

"Get back? Where are you going?" The professor seemed to be full of surprises.

"Oh, yes, I guess with all the excitement I forgot to tell you. I'm going to give a seminar. I'll have to be away for some time, but I know I can depend on you to handle things here. I've arranged for some of the assistants to help you while I'm away. I'm going to give you the codes to access all of the equipment, but remember Celestia; this information is for Your Eyes Only." The professor chuckled at his pun.

As Celestia's seriousness dissolved into an understanding grin, she nodded in agreement and the two scientists continued their work of the day. For a little while, Celestia was too busy thinking about her work. Thankfully, it gave her a rest from thinking so much about Lance.

CHAPTER 10

MORE SCIENCE

The excitement at the laboratory diminished and time began to drag on ever so slowly for Celestia. Work became more and more humdrum. She became quite impatient with her newly assigned assistants, even though she knew the problems that arose were not really their fault. Things were just not the same without Dr. Hall around. They had been able to communicate so well with each other it was like they thought and acted as one. The assistants could not fill that void. Besides, she was lonely, and no matter how hard she tried to communicate with Lance, she always got the same response, 'Unauthorized communication' in a stilted, computerized voice.

No one will listen, no one cares, Celestia fretted. The Source . . . the Source, that's all that's important! What is the Source anyway? Does anyone really know? The Source is supposed to have ultimate knowledge. But then why doesn't the Source care about Lance and me? Celestia felt guilty as such thoughts passed through her mind. She had always been patriotic, but things were getting to her. She couldn't stop resenting the Source, the power that squelched her dreams. In spite of her feelings she was determined to do her job for

Professor Hall and Lance's sake. She kept busy with her work during the day and went out with friends in the evening, but nothing could assuage her loneliness for Lance.

Late one evening at the lab, near quitting time, a young male assistant informed Celestia that they were short of insects, numbers 16 and 23 in biosphere C5. "Since these are needed right away, I'll stay if you need me," he volunteered in a hesitating voice.

Celestia looked up; she forced a smile, knowing the young man had other plans. "You go on. I don't have anything special to do this evening. I'll stay and get them processed."

"Thanks, thanks a lot!" the young man's face brightened at her offer and he quickly turned to leave. As he shut the door behind him, the room was bombarded with dead silence. Celestia poured herself a cup of warm, herbal liquid. She needed something to help her through the evening as she proceeded with the task that she had just taken on.

The evening dragged on as slow as molasses. A talking timepiece finally announced it was 9:30 p.m. The tired scientist was eager to leave the laboratory and began the process of closing up. She went over the checklist of buttons and levers to be pushed and pulled, as methodically as any pilot navigating a space ship would do. The computer was the last item on the list before she would turn off the lights and lock the door of the laboratory. As she reached for the off button, a sudden inquisitiveness gripped her. She wondered what formulas or combinations of formulas Professor Hall had used when he cloned the chimpanzee.

Quickly scanning the computer screen, Celestia laughed to herself at the whole exercise in futility. What good is it? It would be like finding a needle in a haystack, and what good could possibly come from this? Half-heartedly, she scanned through the professor's notes. Hardly taking the time to read enough to understand anything, and being too tired to care, she shrugged, turned off the computer and the lights, locked the door and elevated back to an empty apartment. The silence was deafening and it had her mind wondering. She hadn't heard from Lance, Jane or Alex for quite some time. Where were they? What were they doing? Was Lance even remotely thinking about her? There was no way to know, so she resigned herself to being alone, carrying on the tedious work at the lab. Even though she had assistants, it was not an easy task to move forward without Professor Hall.

CHAPTER 11

EARTH CHANGES

No one knew how many years had passed since the great cataclysm wreaked havoc on the Earth causing continents to shift, smashing them together, changing the configuration of land and sea. Cities of unknown origin were strewn in ruins around the world. There was not much left to make any sense of what had been. There were survivors, people of diverse races and cultures who were thrown together, and after so many years had passed, none of them knew where they had come from. They had no reason to think they had originally come from some distant place. Although they generally managed to get along together, at times there were skirmishes between people for one reason or another. Many had separated into isolated tribes and arguments arose over territory, beliefs, or any number of reasons that can cause people to fight among themselves.

One area of the ruins was called Egyptralia; a name that had been orally handed down from one generation to another since the great cataclysm. The people who occupied the land were called Barbarians, a name that did not originate from their own forbears. It was a name given to them by the Hybridites, a super race with an evil ruler, Zarno. Zarno and his followers kept the so-called Barbarians in bondage by the Hybridite's technological superiority and the lies that were told to them. In spite of being kept in mental and physical bondage, the Barbarians scraped out a living the best they could while serving the superior race of Hybridites. Although they sometimes became rebellious, shouting, "We are not animals!" they helplessly succumbed to the power of Zarno's security police. They were unable to become educated, progress as a people, build cities or grow as a society. They were kept ignorant of any intellectual past and provided no hope for a better future. The Hybridites had advanced transportation facilities built, using Barbarian labor, to speed the workers back and forth in supersonic pods from their dwelling places to work in the splendid cities of the Hybridites. These pods sped over land and water, always under the watchful eyes of the security police. By not giving allegiance to the Source, the Barbarians were not allowed to own businesses; and although they worked long hours, they earned very little in return. Even among the Hybridites, Zarno's government closely monitored every transaction. Because of the Source, the ruling powers virtually owned everything, and there was no need for currency to be exchanged. Everyone received credits, from which the price of any purchase was deducted. If the governing officials didn't like what someone was doing, or if they made trouble in any way, their credit could be confiscated. This, of course, would leave them without the means to buy, sell or do any business at all. The Source and its governing officials had complete control. The Hybridites accepted this economic system as normal, for they had no recollection of any other means for trade and commerce.

Most Hybridites thought of the Barbarians as a sub-race, second-class citizens. The Barbarians, on the other hand, thought it ironic that the Hybridites had such an attitude. Barbarians believed that the Hybridites were split off from their race sometime in the distant past. They reasoned that since both groups were more intelligent than animals, they must have been connected in some way at some point. With the current technologies developed over such a long period of time, the Hybridites lost their connections to their past and their own evolution. Hybridites thought they were from a different species altogether.

The Hybridites believe that Barbarians, although intelligent enough to have speech, were animals. One clear attribute to support this claim was that Barbarians indulged in the physical sexual contact to reproduce, rather than their own method of cultural reproduction. Hybridites took the term culture literally, both mentally and physically. To them it was the only reasonable way and quite appropriate to reproduce only in culture dishes. They could not only design their offspring according to their preferences, they could avoid defects and disease. Because of the ease of their methods of procreating their species, and the fact that their life expectancy was growing longer, the population was mushrooming out of hand. The Hybridite's governing officials preferred to solve this problem by shipping their own unsuspecting people off the earth into space, just like they did with the garbage.

Although the Hybridites left the Barbarians to fend for themselves, many were sympathetic and merciful enough to leave these wretches their discards. Unwanted items would be dropped off near the Barbarians' dwellings in the middle of the night. With no attempt to be sociable, they would hurriedly return to their affluent homes and resume their elitist lifestyle.

Zarno and his government officials tried to squelch any hopes of advancement by the Barbarians; nevertheless, the Barbarians did not wholly give up their natural instincts or their pride. One such man was Alex Carter Taylor. Alex was determined to cooperate with the elders of his people. The elders, or 'Old Ones', were convinced that the Barbarians, as they were called by the Hybridites, originally came from a highly developed civilization. From knowledge handed down from one generation to another, the legends guided Alex to where he and other Barbarians thought the proof they were looking for could be found. Various clues led them to believe that the proof they needed was secretly buried long ago in the sands of Egyptralia. The Barbarians believed that Alex was their greatest hope to uncover the mysteries of their past, and by having him work as an archeologist for the Hybridites, he would find the proof of what they believed was their former heritage.

CHAPTER 12

THE LAND OF THE BARBARIANS

The bronzed arms and shoulders of Alex Carter Taylor glistened with perspiration from the sun that bore down on him and the sweltering sands of Egyptralia. The bearded blonde archeologist threw down his shovel and grabbed a flask of water. He voraciously gulped the cool liquid, and then poured some over his head, catching the drops with the white scarf around his neck.

How much longer is it going to take? Alex thought. If there were any more to be found it would have been found weeks ago. Alex was becoming exasperated. The relics that had already been found weren't proof enough to most of the Barbarians, and would be even much less proof to the Hybridites. They needed more than a few broken shards to be convincing, except to those who sincerely believed they had a better past.

The elders, or the 'Old Ones', as they were called, lived in caves located in the surrounding desert hills. They shunned Zarno's Honorable Order Of The Source. They had directed Alex to an area located in the hot sands, confiding to him that their legends told of that place. They told him he would surely find information, records and artifacts that were buried beneath those sands generations ago. The records and artifacts could prove to both their own people and to the Hybridites that they once had a great civilization; it would also be revealed that the current government of Zarno was evil and suppressed their people from the prosperity that was rightfully theirs.

Alex felt in his heart that the monk-like 'Old Ones' might be right. At times he might doubt that any more evidence would be found. Like the 'Old Ones', however, he could not find it within himself to show allegiance to Zarno's governing power; a power that held a controlling grip on his people and even on the Hybridites. His need for independence would not permit him to tolerate the current predicament of the gullible Hybridites who believed in the government ruled by Zarno and his officials. He would rather live along with the rest of the outcasts, working in the biospheres and bartering among themselves for food and other necessities of life. He felt it better to have hope of finding proof of their true past, than to succumb to a life with no future.

Unknown, but suspected, Alex felt that Zarno and his leaders had no worries about the Barbarian population. He truly believed that Zarno already had plans to subject him and his people to complete slavery after the bulk of the Hybridites were evacuated, and ultimately eliminated. Zarno and his power mongers would have no contest with the helpless Barbarians, so Alex, the 'Old Ones' and the Barbarian race must find a way to overcome the fate that lie ahead.

Alex wanted no part of Zarno's government, yet in the sweltering heat he couldn't help embracing the thought of living an easier life by being more cooperative with the Hybridites, by doing their will and giving up his archeological work. He had important Hybridite friends in high places, like Lance and Celestia, who thought he was more intelligent than most Barbarians. Since Lance was a space pilot and Celestia was a scientist, they had realized Alex's ability. They educated and trained him to work at something better than the work in the biospheres or the menial factory jobs. He didn't have to be out here sweating in this blasted hot sun! Such were his thoughts as he felt the frustration grow from the lack of success in his endeavors. At times, when he began to doubt the validity of the stories he had heard, he'd think Lance was right; that he had been digging upside down. Like Lance, he should be digging to find new worlds in space to explore and inhabit.

This heat must be getting to me, Alex surmised, reprimanding himself for thinking such thoughts. He knew he could never let his people down and he could never bend to the will of the Source or its rulers. At least Alex knew that as long as they did not make outright trouble, those in government positions would not bother him and his people.

Even though harsh times were upon them, the Barbarians had their happier moments. Tonight there was to be a feast and the workers at the dig were let go early in preparation for the festivities. Alex was left alone at the site. Without having to direct others, or hearing the clamor of their clattering shovels and sifting fragments out of the sand, he could possibly get a better perspective of the overall situation.

Resolved to carry on his search for even some small piece of evidence to give credibility to the tales of the 'Old Ones', Alex reached for the shovel he had thrown down. Suddenly a voice interrupted his intentions. He turned, squinting at the blinding sun. If he hadn't heard the voice, he would have thought he was seeing a mirage. The mysterious form from which the voice beckoned was like that of the Egyptian queen, Nefertiti, in the tales he had heard from the 'Old Ones'. As his eyes adjusted, Alex stared at the goddess-like figure emerging from the sun. The figure was even more beautiful as it came into view against the azure sky. He was afraid the apparition might disappear at any moment, when suddenly the spell was broken by laughter.

"Are you going to spend all of your time out here in this scorching sun?" the vision mockingly questioned.

Alex regained his senses, realizing the voice was that of Jane, the orphan he had recently met at California Island. "What are you doing out here?" Alex was outwardly worried for her sake, and nonetheless pleased with her presence. His eyes searched the scraps of fabric she wore that had been left by the Hybridites. Pieced together; they clung to her body in such an enticing way. "You should never have come out here!" Alex scolded.

"Don't you want me around?" she asked tauntingly, yet at the same time sweetly, "Here, I brought you some of the food that was to be served at the festival tonight. A little won't be missed and it's for a good cause" she justified. Alex turned and looked back at the sand and his shovel, knowing he was losing precious quiet time to search for the artifacts needed to uncover.

"I went to all this trouble and what thanks do I get?" Jane pouted.

Alex turned back to looking up at Jane from the pit and conceded, "All right, I'll put up with you, you little thief, but just until after I get my fill of whatever you've got in that basket." Playing along, Alex acted like he was doing her a favor as the two of them made their way to a clear pool surrounded by a shelter of palm trees; a welcome oasis amid the burning sands.

Jane carefully spread a cloth and the delicacies from the basket between them. "Do you really believe you'll find anything out here?"

Alex became serious. "All odds seem to be against it, yet somehow I have this feeling there are still things hidden, just waiting to be uncovered. There's something in me, maybe just hope that drives me, but I have to keep on searching. No one will believe in what the 'Old Ones' say until we have proof, tangible evidence." Alex became silent for a moment. This was no time to go into a heated lecture and spoil Jane's good intentions. His mood softened as he drank in Jane's beauty, as well as the thirst quenching beverage she had provided. He wanted to keep these moments they had together forever. Feeling he would be doing her an injustice by leading her on romantically, he groped for the right words. "Look, Jane, you should not have left Jameripan and I'm going to see that you get back safely. It's not the same here. We're outcasts, living a futile existence. You have a chance to live with a Hybridite family and even though you'll be working for them, at least you'll have a chance for a better life. This is no place for someone like you."

"Oh, Alex, don't you see . . . I can't go back . . . I belong here with you and the rest of our kind. These are my people. I'm not like Celestia, and even if she is my friend, there are too few Barbarians living in Jameripan. I could never adjust to the Hybridite way of life, even if it is easier. I might like to visit once in a while, but I would never really belong. No, even if you don't want me, I'm not going back! Besides, I could help you here at the dig if you really believe what you're doing is so important!" Jane spouted out the words authoritatively. Then she looked up at Alex and as her eyes met his, a smile emerged across her face while she sheepishly asked, "Would you like a fig?" Alex accepted her offering but said nothing. He ate the fig as if he had not been paying any attention to her chatter.

Palm leaves gently swayed, brushed by a gentle breeze. Nearby, tethered camels drank in the cooling waters of the oasis. Alex was passionate in his quest for the truth to be unearthed. He was passionate for the beauty that surrounded him. Most of all, he was passionate for Jane!

In a trance of vivid imagination, Alex recalled the stories told by the 'Old Ones'. Emotions welled up within him as he envisioned, Jane as the beautiful Nefertiti appearing upon the sands, and he was the mighty Akhenaten, the Egyptian king he had heard about in legends. To himself, Alex was the king who swept the beautiful Nefertiti up into his chariot and roamed the desert freely, with her beside him as he performed heroic deeds. Alex's romantic fervor grew along with his imagination. He tossed the fig basket away; he suddenly pulled Jane toward him and pressed his lips tightly to hers as he gently slid the scarf from her shoulders. He explored her neck with kisses, slowly working his way down over her smooth soft skin and breasts. When Jane felt the firm grip of Alex's hand, she noticed how rough his hand was from working at the dig. She didn't care. His strong hand made her feel secure. She felt the rise and fall of her breath as he slowly worked his way down over the curves of her torso and hips. In spite of her better judgment, she would accept his advances. Responding, she loosened the frayed rope belt of his patchwork khaki pants. Her innermost feelings almost prodded her to resist, but not only did the desire to make love with him overpower her senses; it was the longing to belong and to belong to the one man she wanted more than any other, even if it meant giving up her virginity. She had been secretly tortured by the searing pangs of orphanage. Sympathetic people had provided for her basic need for food and shelter since the day she had been found as a child, wandering from one place to another, hungry, dirty, deserted. She had been cared for but never had a deep feeling of belonging to anyone. She was only known as just Plain Jane with no family ties. There was no one to reveal her secret longing to, no one to fill the empty hollow in her heart. She wanted to belong to Alex; she would use any means possible to feel the warmth of his embrace, to hold his love . . . to belong to him.

There was no question that Alex's physical attributes were fully unimpaired. Lost in their desire for one another, the quickening rustle of palm leaves was not heard. For Alex and Jane, time was temporarily forgotten until suddenly, all too soon, a shifting wind and baying camels startled Alex. Aware that the afternoon would quickly dissolve into evening, Alex broke the spell, leaving Jane in puzzling disarray. "We'd better get back to camp," he announced sternly as if nothing had happened. Jane, dizzy from the abrupt change in his attitude, smoldered in anger for being rejected at the moment of their heightened desire. Hurt and disappointed, Jane scrambled to gather the leftover food and threw it into the basket, as she also threw a piercing look of anger at Alex. "What is wrong with you?" she screamed. "Did I do something wrong? You go on without me! I got here by myself and I can get back by myself!"

Alex did not respond to Jane's outbursts. He calmly walked toward her, picked her up while she kicked and screamed as he plopped her on her camel's back. Still angry, she muttered a few more obscenities. Unperturbed, Alex led her camel alongside his. Even while fussing at him, she knew she didn't really want to go back by herself. It would soon be dark.

Heading back to the village, Alex did not attempt to explain his actions. He said nothing. His changed attitude remained the same after their unfulfilled romantic rendezvous along with the wind that had so quickly shifted. As Jane's temper simmered down

somewhat, puzzling thoughts began to take over her disappointment. What had made Alex jump up so suddenly? She knew he was
certainly capable, what could possibly have held him back? Surely,
it would take more than the wind and baying camels to deter him;
and the drums? There was no question, not even the drums should
have brought him up like a drowning man, rising out of the water,
gasping for air. Did he think he was not the first to make love to her?
He had surely seen others make advances toward her, but it hadn't
occurred to her that he might think she had made love with someone
else. Maybe that was it! Now she was angry not only with Alex, but
ashamed of the fact that she threw herself at him and would have to
suffer the consequences. Such thoughts ran back and forth in confusing circles in her mind, until she ultimately denied all of them.
There was something else that bothered him, she was sure of it. What
could it be? What secret could be lurking in his heart to make him
act as he did? As Jane continued to search her mind for what might
bother Alex, she remembered the girl in the village who one day, just
happened to appear seemingly out of nowhere, by his side. That's
it; it must be Priscilla, that pesky blonde who always just happens
to be simpering around wherever Alex is. Pris, they call her, miss
goody two shoes, always flouncing around in a dress with a bow in
the back and wearing a ribbon in her hair; she probably never had to
get her hands dirty. Alex is impressed with Pris, that haughty, snobby
daughter of one of the most influential families in the village. That's
why Alex acts like he does; Jane continued her catty speculations.
He probably intends to marry her! Mixed feelings swirled around
in Jane's mind. She cringed within herself knowing she was thinking
bad things about someone she hardly knew, but she couldn't help it.
She couldn't stand the thought of Alex marrying her.

As Jane pondered Alex's strange behavior, she was surprised, then relieved when he finally broke the silence. "Tomorrow we'll have to get an early start . . . and be sure to wear something more suited for digging!" he ordered in sarcastic tones, fighting his conscience for treating her the way he did and for selfishly wanting her to remain in Egyptralia with him. How could he explain his inner feelings to her? In his mind he was protecting her. He knew he would not make a commitment to her and he dared not try to explain why. She wouldn't understand the reason he had that was locked up in his heart. He hurt her now, but it would only hurt her more, later . . . when he would have to end their relationship.

Jane knew that in spite of Alex's gruffness, he didn't want her to leave Egyptralia after all. He even wanted her to go to the dig with him tomorrow. This was not the time to prod his thoughts. She would have to wait until a better time for that. Her smile developed into the grin of a victor as the two would be lovers, both harboring within themselves secrets they dared not share, turned their camels toward the disappearing sun.

Two lone camels traversed the desert expanse with their riders silhouetted against the orange-red sunset that was diminishing the blue afternoon sky into dusk. Even before they saw the glow of bonfires in the star-studded night, drums were heard beyond the hills. The festivities of the Barbarians were about to begin!

CHAPTER 13

A MYSTERIOUS STRANGER

The Barbarians trickled out from their lodging places. Some came by camel; some came by makeshift wagons and some walked to the celebration. As the Barbarians gathered together on their way to the festivities, it was obvious that their makeshift wagons and clothes were pieced together from the cast-offs of the smaller Hybridites. Each person or family brought whatever food they could contribute. The combined victuals made a bountiful array of hearty fare that was set upon wooden tables. Bright multi-colored awnings covered the tables from scraps of material that had been pieced and sewn together by the women. Unlike the Hybridites whose diet consisted of insects, seaweed, kelp, algae, soy and some vegetable extracts, the Barbarians ate various kinds of meat for which they either hunted or raised by their individually owned flocks. They also had vegetables and fruit that they raised in their own gardens or in the biospheres. The Hybridites let the Barbarians use the biospheres to raise some of their food. They wanted strong healthy workers. The women made breads and cakes from the ground meal they made from grain. In all, there was enough for everyone, even those who could not contribute.

Alex and Jane arrived in time for the feast. They were seated near the elders who had vehemently professed knowledge unknown by the outside world. One of the elders, Apiatan, was a man of reddish complexion and few words. (Apiatan's name was passed down to him through the ages. His family was told that one of his ancestor's was a great chief before the cataclysm). He arose and led a prayer of thanks. "Friends, the world has forgotten the one true Spirit Father. We know we are all of the same blood. Our brothers, the Hybridites, have forgotten the true path. Evil rulers who speak with forked tongue have blinded them. We are fortunate to have among us one who will bring from Mother Earth secrets that have been buried, but now the time has come for those secrets to be revealed. Let us welcome Alex Carter Taylor and his workers who will bring us knowledge of our forgotten past." As Alex stood up, all toasted with their various cups, mugs, and coconut shells in appreciation of Alex and his helpers. What a contrast was this simple ceremony compared to the one given Lance at California Island. These humble, simple people, who hardly had enough for themselves, generously brought their contribution to this meeting in the desert in order to keep Alex and his crew working. Their appreciation and trust in him, as well as his ability to succeed, moved him. He would not trade places with Lance for all the riches of California Island, or for the recognition bestowed on Lance by the devious officials of the Honorable Order Of The Source.

The diverse people of the desert enthusiastically shared their food and conversation. By the time they were filled, the darkened sky was studded with stars. Flames from crackling bonfires rose and receded; the glowing warmth was welcomed in the cool of the desert night. Once again the rhythmic beat of drums sounded, inviting syncopated claps from everyone. Some joined hands and danced in a circle. They danced like children of forgotten places much like the gypsies that had no nation. Soon the better dancers were drawn to the middle of the ring of onlookers who resorted to clapping in time to the music. After a while, even those in the center dispersed as drums announced the entrance of the beautiful, unrivaled Jane. She twirled a sheer veil around her shapely form as she danced to the rhythm of the drums and other primitive instruments. Alex could hardly take his eyes off her until, in the shadows, he sensed that a mysterious stranger was watching him. Alex was curious. He tried to follow the stranger's movements, but in the dark, a turbaned figure quickly slipped from one shadow to another. Alex lost sight of the fleeting intruder as his attention was again caught back to the music, paired with the undulating movements of Jane. To his surprise, she reached out and drew him from the crowd of onlookers to join her. Hesitant at first, but cheered on by the crowd, Alex quickly proved he also was no stranger to the dance. The excited Barbarians stamped their feet and clapped their hands even more. To theirs and the spectator's surprise, Leo, another admirer of Jane, suddenly and without invitation, jumped in to join them in the dance. It became clear he tried to outdo Alex to gain Jane's admiration. Faster and faster, the two men attempted to outdo each other while the crowd cheered them on. The rivals became more determined to be the better dancer, showing off their ability while sneering at each other. As the crowd became excited and started making bets on which would be the better dancer, Jane moved back out of the way. It became obvious that Alex was applauded more than Leo. Finally, a heavy set man, a well-respected spectator, confirmed Alex the winner. Amid loud cheers, Alex's arm was raised in victory. Alex bowed to the audience, and being a gentleman, he turned to shake hands with Leo. Leo however, a beaten man, disappeared when the excited crowd could not contain themselves and joined in the fun. Exhausted, Alex and Jane quietly slipped away from the throng of revelers.

It was late in the evening before the syncopated beat of the drums once again sounded, beckoning the Barbarians to a different kind of entertainment. Families and couples gathered together while the children settled down. The younger ones fell asleep in their parent's laps. Some people sat on broken walls and stones of ancient ruins. Quietness pervaded except for the extra crackling fires that were added to help warm the people from the nighttime cool air, or the distant howls of animals resounding from the hills. Shadows of palm fronds draped across the moon. A large bearded man entered the clearing as drums, flutes, and other primitive instruments brought forth soft melodious music. A strong voice filled the night with song. Loudly, then softly, soulfully, the singer's voice, along with others, reverberated late into the clear night. The last note of the performance seemed to hang in the air as the enraptured audience slowly wended their way by their wagons or other means back to their homes. Arm in arm, Alex and Jane disappeared into the night. As Alex drew Jane closer to him, he didn't want to let her go. His arms encircled her unresisting body. Jane wanted desperately to hear him say the words she had so longed for, but they did not come. She knew he could have any woman he wanted. Yet, he always came back to her. He had told her he loved her, but never offered to marry her. As she looked up at him longingly, she thought how handsome, how strong he was, how noble and responsible he was. He was so dependable in every way, except with her. What was holding him back? She knew better than to press him about the subject for fear of driving him away. Although she knew in her heart that Alex did love her and only her, there was something she didn't know. Alex could not bring himself to admit that he didn't want to marry her because she was an orphan. She didn't have any relatives. He had tried to reason with himself, that it was a foolish reason not to ask her to marry him, but he really wanted to marry someone with a family. How could he tell her that when he had children they would have a grandmother? They would have a sweet grandmother who would bake little cakes and tell stories to them. If he married Jane that would never be. It was something he dared not admit to her or to anyone. Alex was proud. No one suspected that under his manly appearance there was an unresolved soft spot in his heart. He was caught between his own two unforgiving desires. He knew he should stay away from Jane, but he couldn't make himself give her up. Alex temporarily put aside his torturing thoughts. He made certain Jane was safely home, leaving her in her quandary, and then he returned to his own lonely cabin.

Alex needed to sleep so he could get an early start with the others at the dig. He tossed and turned as sleep evaded him. He was obsessed not only by his inability to cope with the problem of Jane, but also by thoughts of the mysterious turbaned stranger who had been watching his every move earlier that night. In spite of forebodings, he finally, though fitfully, drifted off to sleep.

The night had been long and the morning short when sunlight streamed through the cabin window. Alex rolled over, punched his pillow and struggled to get into a more comfortable position. After a few moments he turned and punched the pillow again. He knew it was useless and soon surrendered to the inevitable. He rubbed his hand over the stubble on his chin, pulled on his rope-tied, patchwork pants and lit a makeshift stove to heat a pot of leftover coffee. Coffee was grown in one of the biospheres, one of a few concessions the Hybridites allowed; allowed not only to make it seem they were sympathetic to the needs of the Barbarians, but the stimulant helped boost the workers' productivity. Leftovers of bread, cheese and fruit weren't much for a laboring man's breakfast, but it was quick and easy. As he waited for the coffee to heat, he opened a window and sucked in the cool early morning desert air. He was soon lured back to the table by the smell of the now warmed coffee. While enjoying this last cup, Alex pondered the events of the previous night. First he thought about Jane. How wonderful it would be if she were here now in this lonely cabin. Then his thoughts were yanked back once again to the mysterious stranger. Who was he? Why was he staring at him? Alex's intuition told him that something was just not right. He couldn't figure it out and eventually told himself it was just his imagination. No use worrying about it now, he reasoned. Last night's ceremony had renewed his interest and curiosity about the past and he had resolved to start work on a new section of the dig. Preoccupied by his thoughts, Alex forgot about the near empty pot simmering on the stove. Aroused by smoke and burned coffee he quickly threw a ladle of water in the pot and quenched the fire. He was not about to take a chance of having his cabin destroyed. Jolted out of his daydreams, he hurried to get to the dig before the cool morning air would surrender to the unforgiving afternoon sun.

As Alex continued his search in the desert, Lance continued training for his mission, but Celestia met with an unexpected turn of events. Unknown to him, or any of the other Barbarians, there was an unhappy ceremony occurring in Jameripan.

CHAPTER 14

A NEW BREED

Dr. Noah T. Hall, Beloved Professor the sign read. Celestia was numb with disbelief as tears welled from her large almond shaped eyes. How could he die so soon, so unexpectedly? Celestia's grief for the professor was accentuated by her own predicament. Why did this untimely event happen to her? She was looking forward to his return from the seminar so she could go to Lance and try to make amends with him. If she could just get there somehow! She felt certain she could get around the authorities and see Lance in-person, rather than hear those depressing monotone messages from the mission center.

Now there was no hope. She was needed here more than ever. Celestia paid her respects and went back to her lonely apartment. As the night mundanely sauntered on she felt that she, too, would die; a victim of hopeless disillusionment. Wondering how she would have the strength to carry on in Dr. Hall's place, she tried to console herself. "Don't worry, Professor Hall, somehow I'll manage to keep things going. You'll be with me right here by my side, at least in my thoughts." Still ruminating and exhausted by the strain of it all, Celestia finally drifted off to a comforting sleep.

The next day, Celestia tried to be true to her intentions. She responsibly continued on with her work. Her inner strength seemed to grow even more than she believed possible. The brief time she had been in charge of the laboratory turned out to be the best healing experience for her. Now, she threw herself into her work as never before. She chose the fastest learners, the most dependable of her assistants to train, all so they could later be sent to manage other laboratory complexes. It wasn't long before she was quite pleased about how everything was progressing so smoothly. Celestia thought of how proud the professor would be regarding the fine job she had done in his absence. Sometimes, in her mind, she would converse back and forth with the old man, especially when she had a problem or had done an unusually good job. The better things went, however, the more she thought about her personal life and suffered remorse for not being able to reconcile the misunderstanding with Lance. Torn between the two worlds, Celestia was becoming desperate. She had to decide what to do. Of course she couldn't be in two places at once. Should she stay where she was urgently needed, or go to where her heart pulled her? The dilemma persistently nagged at her. She just had to get to Lance, to the space station before his training was over, or it would be too late. The question that tortured her was how?

With the extra responsibility thrust upon her, Celestia frequently stayed overtime at the laboratory. She needed to know more about the information Professor Hall stored in his computer. One evening, as she was going through his private records, she came to the notes about his cloning experiment. As the perfectionist that he was, he had methodically entered every step of the process. Amused at first, Celestia almost skipped passed the secret procedures. Then an idea crept into her brain. At first she dared not think the unthinkable, but in her desperation she reversed the information and went back to the beginning, reading it carefully again. If a monkey can be cloned and grown at an accelerated rate as professor Hall said, why not a Hybridite? Celestia was shocked at her own thoughts at first, and then she remembered that Professor Hall had stated that the next step would be to clone a Hybridite. Maybe the Professor had left her a solution to her problem after all, Celestia reasoned. Maybe I can be in two places at once!

Using her commitment to her work as an excuse for staying late, Celestia began to carry out her plan alone in the late hours of the evenings. She took cells from her own body, carefully nurtured them according to the notes left by Professor Hall, and watched them begin to grow into what she hoped to be an image of herself. As time passed, the reality of her efforts shocked her; she was not prepared for the result. An exact duplicate of her as a child peered out from the small window of the growth accelerator where before, insects were usually processed. The impact of her incredible feat suddenly hit her. What have I done? Oh, what have I done? She remembered that the professor said the process had not yet been perfected. What could he have meant? She didn't want a duplicate of herself as a child. Frantically, she geared up the growth accelerator and waited until soon, a full-grown image of her now peered out of the window. Celestia was exuberant about her success, as well as wary of the final outcome; she even thought of dissolving the experimental being. Her double continued to stare questioningly at Celestia from the window. Celestia was mortified at the thought of her brash decision to clone herself. Even worse, how ghastly it would be to see another being, especially one that looked like her, be thrust into a vat of dissolving liquid and slowly melt away. She wouldn't . . . She couldn't . . . and . . . She didn't! Mustering up some courage, Celestia carefully opened the door to let her masterpiece out. She cautiously stood back, not knowing what to expect.

"Where am I? Who am I?" the confused clone asked as she looked Celestia up and down. Then, the clone started laughing. It startled Celestia to see an image of herself, especially when the creature was laughing at her. She suddenly recognized that the clone had seen herself in the mirror across the room and was laughing because she was just as surprised to see her double. Before long, both of them laughed, pointing at each other. Celestia stopped laughing when she realized she must be in charge of the situation; she became more serious in spite of being nervously shaken by her brash actions.

"You are a clone, the first clone on earth," Celestia explained matter-of-factly as she regained her composure and tried to show her authority. "I created you from myself and for myself," she announced firmly. "I am going to call you Excella, because you came from one of my cells. I created you for a special purpose." While still shaking within, Celestia bravely continued her explanation and to her relief, the newly cloned Hybridite obediently nodded in agreement.

Celestia had gained control for now over the clone. She was worried and uneasy about hiding Excella, realizing that it would be disastrous if anyone saw her double. She could take the clone to her apartment easily enough in the transportube, but it would be more difficult to keep her a secret after getting her home. While hiding Excella in her apartment, she would have to train her to do her bidding and coach her to follow directions with regard to Lance. When they arrived at the apartment, Celestia quieted her nerves with a glass of calming fluid and gave Excella a good looking over. First she noticed her hair. It was Celestia's natural color as with all Hybridites, reddish brown with a touch of green; it had to be changed. She gave the clone a blonde hair color pill, which was swallowed as directed. Celestia was pleased with the results. So far, so good; now strict orders had to be given. She strutted around Excella in her best teaching manner. Excella eyed Celestia's every movement, turning her head to follow her creator. "Excella, you are definitely not to leave this apartment unless I am with you," Celestia warned. "There will be a time when you can go out on your own, but first you will have to go through some basic training so you can get along in this world. Later, if all goes well, I'm going to send you on a mission." Celestia was not sure Excella understood what she was talking about. "Do you understand, Excella? Do you understand what I'm saying?" Excella hesitated for a few moments, and finally, to Celestia's relief, with eyes shining a happy pink, Excella excitedly responded.

"Mission? What kind of mission?"

Celestia proceeded to explain her predicament concerning the need to continue her work, and her desire to make amends with Lance.

With childlike innocence, Excella was eager to please. "I will help you make up with your lover. It will be such fun!" she squealed.

Celestia was not impressed with Excella's seemingly flippant reaction. She was not in the mood to be casual or funny and became even more serious. "Now remember, Lance will think you are me, the REAL me. When the right time comes, I will give you a letter that will explain everything so everyone will believe you are me on a lecture tour. I have to warn you, Excella, you will only have a limited time to accomplish your mission. You'll have to return periodically, so I can give you the formula that will keep your system going. If you don't return as directed, your body will gradually start breaking down. If that happens…" Celestia didn't finish her sentence. She didn't have the heart to explain the consequences.

"I understand," Excella tried to comfort her creator. "I'll help get you and Lance back together again." Excella was excited and innocently sincere about her upcoming project. She diligently listened and learned quickly under Celestia's careful tutoring.

Finally, the day came when Celestia felt that Excella was ready for the trip. After last minute directions, careful packing and making all of the other arrangements needed, Celestia disguised herself so they would not look alike when her mirror image boarded the shuttle headed for space station XRZ29B.

CHAPTER 15

THE IMPOSTER

"Are you going to the seminar this afternoon?" a familiar voice asked. Lance turned and looked quizzically at his friend, a fellow space pilot, Burt Rogers.

"Are you crazy? If I want some sleep I can find some corner to hide in. Why would I want to go hear some old windbag talk when I'm up to my ears in information as it is?"

"Aw, come on, old buddy, you're going to need the information that's going to be dished out. It has to do with the preservation of life forms or something . . . and besides, I've heard some good lookin' dish is going to tell us all about it, not an old windbag. And if you really want to know the truth, I have to go. I'll need to have someone along to keep me awake! I'll tell you what; if it gets too boring we'll both slip out. That way no one can blame me since you, being a commander, insisted we had other important matters to attend to." With a wink and jerk of his head toward the auditorium to accentuate his intentions, Burt Rogers clinched his sales pitch to Lance.

"Well, all right, but if it's too bad we're leaving and you'll have to buy the drinks!" Lance replied as they turned to walk to the auditorium entrance.

"It's a deal!" The two officers shuffled among the noisy crowd while aiming for seats at the end of a row in case they decided to leave before the lecture was over. Since they had to stand up to let late-comers into the row, they had barely gotten settled and didn't hear the introduction. The lights dimmed on the audience, the stage lit up, and a lone young lady appeared at the podium. She fidgeted nervously. The audience's attention became fastened on the beautiful blonde speaker trying to regain her composure. Excella was so nervous the papers of her speech began to shake. She set them down on the podium and looked out at the vast audience full of dignitaries and other important Hybridites. One of the stagehands beckoned for her to begin her speech. The restless audience began to wiggle in their seats as they waited for her to speak. Frozen with fear, she wondered how Celestia could possibly have had the nerve to give a speech like she was told to do in Celestia's place. She wanted to run but alas, the spotlight was on her. Looking around with no alternative in sight, there was nothing else for her to do. Finally she stuttered a few words. Someone yelled "Louder! Could you please turn up the volume?" Excella hesitated, and then attempted to speak again.

"Uh . . . ca . . . can you hear me now?" She hesitated again, and not waiting for an answer, she tried speaking louder. No one hollered for her to speak up again, so after a few sentences the words came easier. Finally, much to her surprise, the rest of the speech seemed to pour out of her mouth effortlessly. She even began to enjoy being in the limelight and thought in confident awe, I didn't know I had it in me!

"Holy Source!" Lance cried out a little too loud as he got a good look at the girl. "She looks just like Celestia! Let me see a program!" Not having one available, he grabbed the program from the person sitting next to him. He didn't bother to apologize to the stunned stranger, and ignored the hushes that surrounded him and Burt Rogers as he read the introduction.

DR. CELESTIA STEVENS
Executive Director and Guest Speaker
Subject: Destiny of the Species

Lance could hardly believe his eyes. Without any warning, sure enough, there she was. He squirmed in his seat, trying to ignore the stares caused by his annoying behavior, then quickly muttered a thank you as he handed the program back to the befuddled stranger. He wondered if Celestia was going to try to see him, or if still angry with him, would she just give him an icy stare and turn away. Had she gotten over him so easily? Maybe she had met someone else and he was simply a discard. Such thoughts jumbled through his mind. He couldn't stand it any longer. "Come on, let's get out of here!" This time those surrounding him and Burt welcomed his words, even if they were officers. Lance got up while Burt shrugged and smiled at the irritated audience; he was happy to have the opportunity to leave since his admission ticket proved he had attended the lecture.

"I need that drink now," Lance pouted. The two officers entered a room where drinks were served. After several glassfuls they both commiserated emotionally about Lance's plight and females in general.

When Excella finished her speech she felt disoriented. Even though she carried off her impersonation of Celestia brilliantly, it almost made her a nervous wreck and the worst part of her charade was yet to come. She didn't have the slightest idea of how to get in touch with Lance. If and when she found him, would he suspect anything? How could he? Only Celestia and she herself knew anything about cloning. "I'll find him and everything will work out just fine!" she told herself as her innocent optimism returned. I will try to find Lance, but first I could use a drink she decided, belying her own confidence.

Excella approached an usher for directions, and then proceeded to the cocktail lounge. Still unsure of herself in a strange place, she didn't look up while making her way to an empty table. When the waiter approached, she tried to be as calm as possible and ordered a drink.

"I'll have a pink relaxer. . . and, oh, a small order of algae-cakes." Unbeknownst to her, she was not far from where Lance and Burt were sitting. She nervously glanced around the room before she calmed herself down enough to think about what to do next.

In the meantime, Lance and Burt were discussing the coincidence of how the speaker looked so much like Celestia. Burt happened to look up and got a glance of the woman sitting at the table by herself. He moved his head around to get a better look, as he couldn't believe his eyes. He nudged Lance.

"Don't look now ol' buddy, but there's tonight's speaker at that table over there. You were right; she sure does look like Celestia."

Lance casually turned to look so he wouldn't be obvious, but his casualness turned into shock. "That is Celestia! Why didn't she tell me she was coming here?" He was beside himself at the thought of being ignored. Having had a few too many drinks, he got up, approached the unsuspecting Excella and spouted "Well!" Trying to act indifferent, Lance betrayed his feelings by swaying and talking too loudly. He was not concerned that his behavior was not befitting an officer. "I see you don't talk to ol' friends" he slurred sarcastically.

Burt tried in vain to coax Lance to leave, making a desperate attempt to avoid trouble and an embarrassing scene. Lance pulled his arm away abruptly and waited for a response from the woman he thought was Celestia.

"Come on Lance, let's go somewhere else" Burt again pleaded, hoping to evade attracting attention.

Wide eyed, Excella perked up when she heard Lance's name. "Oh, Lance, I've been meaning to find you!" she chirped excitedly.

"Oh, sure, sure, I've been meaning to find you" Lance mimicked her in a high voice. "That's why I never heard from you" he added cynically.

Excella looked at Burt and he looked back at her as they both shrugged hopelessly. They realized Lance was too drunk to make good sense out of anything, but Excella tried anyway.

With her best impersonation of Celestia, Excella pleaded with Lance. "Believe me, I tried to call, I tried to write, but every time I tried I only got a response of 'Classified Information' from a speaker. Oh, Lance, I didn't have to give this seminar. It was the only way I could get past the authorities." Fearing that someone might overhear her, Excella lowered her voice to a whisper. Burt sensed Excella's secrecy, and being afraid that Lance was in no condition to be quiet, he coaxed the two out of the room. "Come on, we'll settle this somewhere else."

After a brisk walk, Lance's drinks began to wear off. "You mean you really did try to contact me?" he asked hopefully, much like a little boy.

"Of course I did" Excella soothed.

Burt could see that Lance and the woman he thought was Celestia were making up, so he conveniently slipped away unnoticed. Suddenly, Excella became aware of Burt's absence and realized she was alone with Lance. Now she felt vulnerable and became nervous thinking he would notice something different about her. He might even try to make advances. She didn't know what to do and it was obvious that she was uncomfortable.

"What are you so nervous about?" Lance asked as he noticed her fidgeting.

Startled, Excella jumped a bit. "Oh, I . . . I guess I'm. Well, I guess I thought you might not like me anymore" she muttered for lack of not thinking of a better excuse. Seeing that Lance accepted her fabricated reason, she smiled and tried to relax, content that she had found a suitable answer.

"Like you? Like you?" he repeated, "No, I don't like you, I love you!" he eagerly responded.

"Oh, Lance, you make me so happy!" Excella sighed with relief. She began to feel more confident now that Lance believed her excuse. As Lance took her hand and drew her close to him, she searched for a way to stave off his advances without making him suspicious of her real identity. At the same time, however, she noticed how strong and handsome he was. She trembled as he bent down to kiss her. What would Celestia think? This wasn't part of the plan. Her thoughts raced within her. Excella knew that, in spite of her feelings, Celestia gave her specific directions. She was not to let Lance touch her in any way! Excella, being mindful of her training, gently pushed Lance away. He looked at her in wonder of what he did wrong. Not wanting to antagonize Lance, Excella had to think quickly.

"I'm sorry, Lance, I do love you, but I need time. It's been so long since we've been together . . . and I'm so tired. It's all been such a strain lately."

Lance laughed. "I don't know what's gotten into you, but if that's the way you want it." His sentence broke off as his countenance became more serious. Though perplexed, he wasn't going to ruin a good thing. "Sure, you've had a rough day, sweetheart, I'll walk you back to your suite. You get a good night's sleep and I'll see you in the morning." Lance drew Excella close once more. Excella held her head down trying to avoid any further confrontation, but curiosity got the better of her. Slowly she raised her head and looked up into his eyes.

"Remember, Celestia, whether you will be thinking about me or not, I won't stop thinking about you." Lance poured his compelling spell over Celestia's imposter, and then turned away leaving the poor clone in a state of bewilderment.

Alone in her room, the love-stricken impersonator sat on the edge of her bed. Contemplating the events of the day, she rationalized to herself. This was certainly not what she and Celestia had planned. Who would have guessed that she, too, would fall in love with Lance Locke? But of course it was only natural. Wouldn't she, having been created from Celestia's own cells, be prone to like what she liked? Then it wasn't her fault; it was bound to happen. Oh, why hadn't Celestia thought of that before sending me on this stupid mission?

Excella took the letter Celestia had given her out of her purse and re-read it. She reasoned that once she gave the letter to Lance, it would be all over for her. Lance would see the reason for this charade. He would see that she was only a messenger and who knows what would happen after that? Why, she might even be dissolved like the helpless cloned insects! Excella couldn't bear the thought of it. Besides, her attraction to Lance was too strong. As if in a daze, she stared at the letter again for a few moments, trying to figure out what to do. Remembering the invigorating liquid heat gun that was furnished in her suite, she held it up to the letter and watched the paper crinkle up and disappear in flames. She was amazed at her own boldness. It was almost like burning herself, for she knew that she had also scorched her relationship with her maker. Torn between her desire to carry out her mission and her own desire to be with Lance, Excella was too upset to sleep. She tossed and turned fitfully, trying to justify her actions. She had been given life she reasoned, why shouldn't she also have love? Eventually, she drifted to sleep while imagining that Lance loved her. He would belong to her, not to Celestia!

Lance had also returned to his room. He, too, was bothered by his thoughts. He still wondered about the woman he thought was Celestia. His parting words to her were that he would not stop thinking about her. He thought about probing the sleeping Excella's mind, but it was no use. No matter how much he wanted to, he only drew a blank. He surmised that his advances might chase her away forever. So, he regretfully gave up, turned off the light and wondered if being in love would always be this difficult. He went to sleep still unaware that Celestia was not really there.

The next morning Excella woke early. Feeling refreshed, she was bubbly with excitement since she had settled on her intentions for herself and Lance. In her naiveté, now that she had freed herself from all responsibility to Celestia, she would enjoy her stay at space city XRZ29B. She would surprise Lance. She would wake him early so they could spend the morning together.

Humming to herself, Excella showered with golden light and rummaged through her few pieces of clothing. Wanting to impress

Lance, she settled on a little too tight, low cut, bright red blouse to pair with the gray pants of the business suit she wore yesterday. To her, the gray suit was drab and the red blouse would certainly appeal to Lance. She was busily fixing her hair when she noticed darker roots showing beneath the blonde. She pulled the top of her hair apart to see how bad it looked. *That's funny. I was sure my blonde pills would last longer.* She ran back into the bedroom and tossed clothes about from her suitcase, frantically looking for more hair color pills. Surely Celestia wouldn't have forgotten to pack those for her! None were to be found. She went back to the mirror and looked again, hoping the dark roots wouldn't be too obvious. On closer inspection she noticed her skin was already showing some wrinkles, too. Before long there would be more and her skin would begin to sag. *I can't let Lance see me this way,* she thought. She was almost panic-stricken. *Damn Celestia!* She was afraid something like this might happen. Excella was certain that Celestia planned this to make sure she wouldn't stay here too long!

Excella paced the floor trying to think of a solution, but it was no use. She had to go back to Earth . . . back to Jameripan . . . back to the laboratory and Celestia. Facing the inevitable, she decided to write a note to Lance while he was still sleeping. Groping for the right words, she began, *Dear Lance, I had an emergency call and it was imperative that I leave at once. I'll be back as soon as possible. I can't explain now, but please darling, wait for me. I love you.* Excella signed the note with Celestia's name. She slipped the note under Lance's door and reluctantly caught the next shuttle back to earth.

CHAPTER 16

GIRLS WILL BE GIRLS

When Excella returned to Jameripan, Celestia met her at the shuttle station and gave the fading clone a dose of the renewing serum she needed. Celestia was eager to hear any news about Lance. "How is he? Did everything go all right? Did he believe you were me? Did you give him my note? Tell me everything!"

"Oh, he was fine. All went as planned and he didn't have any idea about me. He thought I was you, and yes, I gave him your note and he understood everything." Excella sighed and wiped her arm across her forehead in relief as the life giving serum took effect. Regaining her confidence, Excella brushed her hair back while blatantly lying. "I only got to see him long enough to give him your letter. He's expecting you to come back soon." She added a little truth, and at the same time kept the door open for herself to return to the space city.

Unaware of Excella's devious intentions, the girls seemed to be closer than ever with their mutual secret plan. Celestia was so pleased with Excella's report she even took the clone with her to the laboratory when she was sure no one else would be around. Excella had her own secret plan, however, to learn all she could about where the life giving serum, ingredients and precious life giving directions were kept. Celestia was trustingly impressed by her clone's interest. It was something she would later regret.

"I'm going to make your doses of serum stronger for you," Celestia offered. In a motherly tone of voice, Celestia explained she could not keep Excella in hiding forever. "We're going to have to find another place for you. One of the space stations will be suitable where no one would know me, or suspect anything about you being a clone. With larger doses of serum you will be fine for a long time and we can meet when needed to keep you in top condition. In the meantime, I will work on discovering the combination of ingredients that will last a lifetime for you. Apparently, that was what Professor Hall meant when he said his experiment wasn't perfected. He was still trying to find a life extending serum for clones when he died."

Excella was relieved to know that Celestia was not going to disintegrate her like the insects. If Celestia could give her life extending serum, she might be able to find a lifetime amount and further her chances with Lance. She slyly watched Celestia's every entry on the computer, hoping she would see and be able to retrieve the information Dr. Hall had left. Whenever Celestia stepped out of the room for a few minutes, she scanned the information, and then quickly fled back to where she had been before Celestia returned. True to her course, Excella found out how to gain access to the storage room where the cloning compounds and life giving serum were stored.

One day Excella nearly found the final necessary code numbers she was after. She had come up behind Celestia quietly, like a cat. Being intently engrossed with her work, Celestia did not notice that Excella was right behind her. When she finally became aware of Excella's presence she was startled and suddenly jerked around in surprise. Excella quickly covered her actions by handing Celestia a cup of hot nourishing liquid and with a fake smile excused herself. "I'm so sorry I startled you" she whined. "You've been working so hard I thought you might need this." Celestia immediately changed the information on the screen. She didn't think Excella was there long enough to see how much information Excella had seen. Fooled, she accepted Excella's offer of the refreshment, relaxed and leaned back sipping the hot liquid.

Excella had just barely lost the opportunity of reading the information she so badly needed. She forced herself to look cheerful as Celestia began talking between sips of her beverage.

"You know, Excella, we have been working way too hard." Celestia slowly took another sip of the hot brew before continuing. "I think we should have a special dinner tonight and just relax. I've tried to put my work first, but now that I know Lance still cares for me I'm ready to turn more responsibility over to my assistants." Celestia emphasized her feelings by getting up and pacing around the lab. She threw her arms up in disgust. "I'm just so fed up with this work. I want to get on with my life. Somehow, I've just got to find a way to see Lance!"

"But Celestia, you're doing such a wonderful job here," Excella countered. "Just look at everything you've accomplished!" Of course Excella only wanted her rival to remain earthbound as long as possible. Realizing her time in the lab might be short, she stealthily hid some of her belongings in order to have an excuse to come back later. Unaware of Excella's actions, Celestia drew one more sip from her cup before suggesting they go back to the apartment for dinner. Without any sign of betrayal, Excella helped Celestia go through the closing checklist. Excella intently observed the motions Celestia used to lock up before they took the transportube back to Celestia's apartment.

Feeling confident of Excella's good intentions, Celestia wanted to make her clone feel at home. "Let's see, what would be better, seaweed soufflé, kelp casserole or soyloin steak?" She rattled off some of the vegetables and sea harvested plants, the usual items of the meatless diet of the Hybridites. Unlike Celestia's happy mood change, Excella rolled her eyes in disgust at her failure to get the coveted information she wanted.

"You choose, Celestia. I'm not familiar with everything. I'll probably like whatever you like."

"I'm going to change into something more comfortable first," Celestia called back on her way to the bedroom. She didn't realize how true Excella's statement was about liking what she liked as she called out to Excella, who was still in the kitchen. Excella was nervously preoccupied, wondering how to get to the computer since she had memorized the code for the life-giving clone serum. The last thing on her mind was what they would have for dinner. She had to think quickly. "Oh, no, I left my essentials belt in the lab," Excella whined, emerging from the kitchen.

Trying to be accommodating, Celestia yelled back. "Oh don't worry; you can use my things tonight."

Excella didn't expect to hear that. Her hopes fell, momentarily. She just had to come up with some excuse to get back to the lab. "Oh, darn, I also left the information you wanted me to study back in the lab and I really wanted to read it tonight before I go to bed."

Celestia was impressed with Excella's eagerness to learn and Excella was relieved when, just as she hoped, Celestia's guard was down.

"Well, don't get upset." Unaware that Excella had so intently watched her lock the laboratory door, Celestia showed the motions that Excella already knew. "You go get your notes and I'll fix supper, but hurry; it shouldn't take long. I'm not going to tell you what we're having. It'll be a surprise."

Quickly, Excella seized her opportunity. She hurriedly entered the transportube and zoomed to the lab. Accessing the information bank, she found that it was more complicated than she had remembered and lost track of the time she was taking. Meanwhile, Celestia sat in front of the cold dinner, her festive mood dampened. What was taking so long? I shouldn't have let Excella go alone. Maybe she couldn't open the door, or maybe she couldn't find where she left her things. Numerous reasons buzzed around in Celestia's head until finally it dawned on her that there might be trouble. She decided to go there and see what was going on. She emerged from the transportube and entered the lab. She tried to stay calm and give Excella the benefit of the doubt, but her intuition was soon to be confirmed. The room was dimly lit except for a light shining over the information bank with the lone figure of Excella sitting in front of it.

"You little sneak!" Celestia's voice broke the silence. "What the hell do you think you're doing?"

Excella jumped, startled out of her wits. Realizing Celestia was on to her scheme, the pressure was too much and she broke her silence. "Do you think I want to be at your mercy forever?" she "shouted back angrily. "I'm just trying to find out how to keep myself alive!"

"You ungrateful little . . ." Celestia was at a loss for words momentarily. "You ungrateful package of unfrozen cells!"

"Package of unfrozen cells, am I?" Excella shouted back. "Well, I'll tell you something. You played the almighty creator when you made me for your own selfish purposes, and you got more than you bargained for. Your former boyfriend Lance is now in love with me and I intend to keep it that way!" The truth was out of Excella's mouth before she could think about what she was saying. It was too late. She was mortified to think of the possible consequences.

Celestia was infuriated at Excella's confession. There was no choice of fight or flight for Excella. She had to fight. They grabbed each other and wrestled, pulling hair, kicking and screaming insults. Celestia threatened "I won't give you anymore serum and you'll fade away like last summer's roses! I'll throw you in the clone dissolving solution!" That was exactly what Excella feared.

"Don't count on it!" Excella garbled through gritted teeth. "I already have the formula for the serum and you'll be dead! No one will ever know I'm not you!" The two scuffled like maddened cats until exhausted. They could hardly stand or lift their arms in battle any longer. Their hair, wet with perspiration, hung like strings down in front of their faces. Their clothes, now torn to shreds, barely hung on their bodies. Exhausted, they finally limped and crawled away from one another to gain a moment of recuperative rest.

A couple of moments were all that was needed before the mirror images came to the realization that neither of them could win this battle; it was like fighting with oneself. They were too much alike, having the same build with the same strength, along with the endurance and the will to win. Celestia lay on the floor with her shoulders and head leaning against the wall. Her mouth was bleeding. Her head drooped to one side as she mumbled to the other half conscious Excella, who was sprawled face down where she had crawled before collapsing.

"I've got an idea," Celestia muttered through her swollen mouth.

"Not another one!" came Excella's curt reply. "What's your great idea this time? Haven't you caused enough trouble already?" The worn-out clone managed to squeeze the words out in a painful slur as she covered a blackened eye with her hand.

"We're going to clone Lance!" Celestia announced.

"Sure!" Excella rolled her large almond eyes in disbelief.

"Well, it's either that or one of us has to go permanently, and it's not going to be me!" Celestia stated defiantly.

"Mm hmm" was the only response Excella could generate to her exhausted double.

The two bedraggled women slowly gathered enough strength to get back to the apartment where their cold dinner sat on the table uneaten. It, too, looked rather pathetic by this time. Bypassing the kitchen the battered women fell moaning across their beds. At that moment nothing in the world was as important to them as sleep.

CHAPTER 17

THE DEAL

Celestia, and Excella, bruised and puffy faced, sulkily eyed each other from across the breakfast table. Celestia broke the dreaded silence with the plan to clone Lance.

"It'll never work," Excella doubtingly retorted.

"Oh, come on now, it's got to work. After all, they say two heads are better than one. Especially if they're both like mine," Celestia quipped, attempting to brighten things up. "We've got to figure out how to get Lance back to earth so we can clone him."

The identical Hybridites stared at their plates, dawdling with their breakfast as they tried to muster up a solution. Between silences, they frantically spouted ideas at each other, ideas which they agreed, wouldn't work.

"Lance couldn't leave the space station in the middle of his training. If they didn't work fast, he would be well on his way to another planet. Who knows where that might be or if he will even arrive safely? He could be out there anywhere, maybe lost in space." Celestia gasped frantically at the idea.

"We . . . ll," Excella slurred. "Remember, there are two of us. After all, that's why I'm here, isn't it?" Excella became excited with an idea. "I could take a shuttle back to the space station and get the needed cells from Lance . . . without him knowing, of course. Then you and I could meet somewhere, and you could take the cells back to the lab, and . . . Voila! You create Lance's clone!" Excella beamed with pride, certain that she had figured out the perfect solution.

"Wait just a minute; I don't think so! Not after what happened last time I let you go" Celestia argued.

"Okay, if you want me to stay here and take over the laboratory, it's alright with me." Excella was smugly confident, knowing full well Celestia would never agree to that. "Come on, Celestia, it'll be different this time. After all, we'll both be getting what we want. You'll have Lance and I'll have his clone. We'll all be happy. Lance will gain a twin brother and I won't have any reason to try to get Lance away from you. It's the perfect solution." Excella shared her idea as if it was just good common sense.

"Well, that's true," Celestia conceded, "But now wait a minute! You are not my sister and things are getting a little out of hand here!" She tried to think of another solution, and to Excella's delight, she couldn't. "Alright," Celestia finally agreed, "But we're going to have to agree on one thing. When all of this is over, you and Lance's clone are going to have to go live on another space station, far away from here, so no one will ever find out about this cloning business. Is it a deal?"

"It's a deal!" Excella enthusiastically agreed as the girls shook hands on their pact. The two heads, that are better than one, made final plans for their unusual rendezvous. Lance already expected Celestia to return because of the note Excella had left, but how to get around the authorities? This could be a problem. A seminar could not be used as an excuse this time. Excella would have to disguise herself and go as a potential transferee to XRZ29B. Once she completed her mission, she could say she wanted to go to a different station with someone. That someone, of course, would be Lance's clone. Then Excella and Lance's clone could be free to live their own lives without interference from anyone, even from Lance and Celestia. Celestia was still somewhat skeptical, yet in Excella's eyes the deal was perfect!

CHAPTER 18

NORTH SIDE PASSAGE

The following day Celestia argued with herself about the pact she had let Excella talk her into. How in the world did she get so tangled up in the situation she was in? On the other hand, what choice was there? Should she try to forget Lance? How would that be possible? The thoughts rambled on in her head. She had plenty of chances to marry someone else. Someone like that business tycoon she had dated before she met Lance. She would be on easy street and not have to put up with those space jaunts Lance continually had to go on. Try to reason as much as she wanted to, she always came to the same conclusion. There was no one like Lance. He was a Hybridite's Hybridite. The male Hybridites respected him; even liked him, and the female Hybridites would give anything to be in her place. That is, of course, providing Lance still loved her after their tempestuous fiasco.

Celestia gave in to the fact that there was no alternative. She loved Lance and that was that! Time was of the essence. She would have to act, act quickly and decisively. Now that she had made up her mind, she began to put her plan into action. Her trip would be a dangerous one, so she had to be mentally and physically prepared for it. Of course, she would also have to be properly dressed for the occasion. As she began to pick out her clothes for the adventure, her roboputer, Roberta, became quite upset. It started sputtering, garbling along with a few understandable words trying to get Celestia to change her mind.

Celestia became impatient with Roberta's nagging. "I'm going, and that's that, so stop fussing and go do something productive. Dust the shelves or something. Just leave me alone!" Roberta stopped sputtering, stood still for a moment, and then turned away like a reprimanded puppy. Celestia felt bad for yelling at Roberta, but nevertheless went about selecting clothes for her mission. She chose a black tight fitting pantsuit, matching boots and a leather jacket with silver studs. A black brimmed hat pulled down over part of her face to hide her identity completed her outfit. She was ready for action!

It was dark. Rain splattered on Celestia's sky-skimmer that was parked on the side of the building next to her apartment. After boarding, Celestia made some adjustments to the controls. The craft slowly lifted straight up. The mechanism was maneuvered by the precision of her eye contact. At the desired elevation, the sky-skimmer accelerated to a high speed and headed directly for its destination, the shop of 'Thrifty Sam the Transfer Man'. The shop was located in an old, almost uninhabitable, run-down complex in a remote area some distance from Celestia's ultra-modern city.

As Celestia sped along she could see fields of biospheres and other self-contained complexes similar to hers. Upon approaching her final destination, she had to be careful to dodge the watchful automatic police scanners; the eyes of the government officials. This was the forbidden territory that her former boyfriend had told her about and she did not want to sound off any alarms. Her scanner detectors helped, but were not altogether fail-safe. This was outlaw territory, where the mobsters of the day congregated, and she did not want her reputation ruined by being caught there. She had been warned to stay away, but now she had to see if there was any truth in what her former boyfriend told her. She had to take the chance that this place did exist and sure enough, it did. Upon getting closer, she began looking for a good place to land. Looking over the area she decided to land on the North Side. In her mind it seemed like it would be the safest, if in that forsaken hell-hole, there would be any safe area. It also looked creepier than what she had been told, causing her to have second thoughts about landing. The old city seemed to be just a mass of ghost like remnants of buildings. Reluctant to give up, she scanned the area and carefully lowered her craft to get a better look. This was no place to be if one could help it. The run down complex, as she was told by her ex-boyfriend, was suspected of underground and black market dealings. As much as she dreaded being there, it was the only place she knew of where she might be able to get the illegal transfer needed to get Excella up to space station XRZ29B.

Celestia tried to spot the storefront that had been described to her. She flew through several streets looking over the dingy, decrepit business places, with grimy film covering the remaining unbroken windows. Since she made the trip in the dark for safety's sake, she had to use her own light with extreme caution as she searched the buildings. In spite of her fear, she felt it was fortunate that her former boyfriend had told her about this place. At the time, she didn't believe such a place existed, and now she realized he had been telling the truth. She wondered why the government had let this area go and become so downgraded.

Turning her attention to the task at hand, Celestia's final destination came into view. "Let's see, oh yes, that's it!" Celestia breathed a sigh of relief, knowing she had found Sam's place. She landed safely without being seen, at least as far as she knew, although not as close as she would have liked. Now she would have to walk the rest of the way through dark alleys, boarded up rat infested buildings and try to avoid anyone who might be lurking in the shadows. She gathered all the nerve and strength she could muster and started walking toward the targeted store. Her hand grasped the disintegrator gun at her side. She hadn't gone but a few steps when suddenly, she was scared out of her wits by a rat running across her path. At first she didn't know what it was. She fired at what she thought might be a robber before she saw the rat scurry off. When she realized what had happened, she tried to calm herself. Several more rats ran in her direction; this time she was ready for them. Robbers or rats, she wasn't about to take any chances. Zap, zap, she was successful in hitting two of the rats while others fled. Shaken, she stopped momentarily to regain her courage. Just as she felt calm enough to go on, the wind blew an old piece of wet newspaper against her face causing her to dodge in fright into a doorway. Every few steps seemed to take forever, but she finally reached the old building she was looking for. She cautiously lifted a rusty, iron doorknocker and rapped it lightly against the door. A few moments that seemed like several minutes went by, as she stood in the rain nervously waiting for someone to answer the door. She rapped again, this time harder. Finally a stubble whiskered, unkempt man in an old coverall opened the rickety door, which miraculously remained on its hinges. The grisly proprietor stared at Celestia. Not volunteering a word of greeting, he continued to stare at her with a scowl on his face.

Celestia stood, waiting, and with no other communication from the man, spoke up. "I . . . I . . . need a transfer." Celestia spoke quietly, almost apologetically. She was not sure if the gross man would slam the door in her face or even worse, drag her in. "I need a transfer to a space station," she repeated. "I was told I could get one here."

The man's gruff voice shot out at her "Who told you?"

Shaking within, Celestia bravely managed to tell him her former boyfriend's name. The door slowly squeaked open wider and the grubby looking man gestured for Celestia to enter. Frightened, she cringed at the disheveled, dusty room and foul smell confronting her. She obediently and cautiously complied with his bidding. Once again, without speaking, the proprietor, Sam, motioned with arm outstretched, his fingers wiggling toward himself. Celestia did not have to ask what he wanted; she reached in her waist pack and drew out a silk covered box of jewelry. Although she hated giving up some of her prized possessions, it was well worth it to get Lance back. After taking a closer look at the contents through a jeweler's eyepiece, a nod of approval was granted while Celestia watched in hopeful anticipation. Expressionless, Sam slowly reached under some so-called wares that were used as a cover-up of his real business dealings and pulled out a metal box. He then nonchalantly pulled out some transfer papers and stamped them to authenticate there use. The whole process was, in reality, a sham unbeknownst to Celestia or any other law abiding Hybridite. Those in power would just turn their heads, secretly exacting a fee from the black market dealers for themselves.

Having been formerly oblivious to the evil manipulations of a corrupt system, Celestia felt guilt pangs as she slipped the transfer papers into her pack and dashed through an unrelenting rain to the safety of her sky-skimmer. The worst was over. All she needed to do now was to get by the scanners. If those went off, a robotic police force would be after her. She used every ounce of ability she could muster to dodge the dreaded scanners. She was nearly frozen with fear. She didn't dare look back as she swerved her sky-skimmer in and out between the old buildings to avoid them.

Unknown to her, however, the robotic police had been aware of her all the time. They had watched her for a few moments before they simply turned back to their game of hyper-dimensional spherical chess.

Celestia felt an unwarranted pride and relief for having skillfully dodged the scanners. In reality, no one really cared. For her, this secretive trip was a huge success. Still somewhat shaken by the ordeal, Celestia breathed a sigh of relief and tried to relax as she headed home with the prized transfer papers.

CHAPTER 19

THE RENDEZVOUS

Excella preened in front of a mirror, wearing one of Celestia's tight-fitting, less sedate outfits. Her long blonde hair fell over her shoulders as she turned her head and dipped up and down, trying to see how she would look from the back, as well as the front. "What do you think?" she mistakenly asked Celestia.

"It's a little bold for travel, don't you think?" Celestia answered with a razor sharp question. "Now Excella, don't forget what you're going on this trip for, and whatever you do, don't let Lance read your mind or the whole deal is off. You'll end up where you started; you'll be just a bunch of disjointed cells!"

"Oh Celestia, you're such a wet blanket! Why don't you loosen up? You're so serious all the time. Don't you ever have any fun?"

This time the question went unanswered; Celestia pretended not to hear. "Come on, we'd better get going or you'll miss the shuttle." Excella did hit a sensitive spot, for Celestia knew there was a lot of truth to the barbing remarks. She began thinking how true it was that she had been too serious about her work and didn't really have much fun anymore. By watching Excella, it was as if she was seeing another side of herself that had been forgotten. She had felt so responsible regarding her career. She had lost sight of the childlike qualities Excella displayed so naturally. Perhaps the happy-go-lucky attitude that Excella displayed wasn't total flippant irresponsibility after all. Maybe it was a part of her own suppressed personality, which gave others the impression she was a 'cool cookie'. Come to think of it, she did have more fun before she became so involved in the lab and obsessed with working for the Cause. Not only that, after her terrible experience regarding her trip yesterday, she was a little suspicious of the governments neglect of that part of the city. Maybe she was too naive, thinking things were more perfect than they really were. Perhaps she could learn from Excella, how to loosen up a little, and Excella could certainly learn to use a little more restraint from her.

Celestia turned her attention back to the mission at hand. She would have to take Excella to the shuttle in order to make sure everything went smoothly. She decided she would have to wear a disguise; it would not do to have two of her and have to explain to the authorities. She wished she was going instead of Excella. She would gladly have it the other way around, especially after seeing how blatantly and boldly Excella was dressed. Realizing there was no other choice, Celestia donned a cape, sunglasses and covered her hair. The two would go as mother and daughter. With their respective parts rehearsed, they hurried to the shuttle station.

Excella enjoyed mocking her creator by putting on an act for the benefit of the inspectors and other passengers at the shuttle station. "Goodbye, mother, I'll miss you!" she called back. She waved as Celestia cringed with disgust at the exaggerated act that Excella was enjoying. It was too much for comfort and Celestia reluctantly waved back. Relieved to see that Excella was finally on her way, she went home to nervously await the outcome of Excella's rendezvous with Lance. Well, at least it won't be much longer if everything goes well, she told herself in an attempt to keep her spirits up. Before long, she reasoned, Excella and Lance's clone will be off to another space station and the whole crazy matter will be over. Then at last she and Lance will be free to get on with their lives.

Thoughts of the future concerned Celestia. How much time could they have together? If Lance is going to another galaxy, when would he come back, if at all? Doubts nagged at her. She knew, however, that even a little time with him was better than none and she would have to make herself believe that he would either not go, or would return safely. In the meantime, she reasoned, she would just have to prepare her assistants as best she could to carry on her work. Celestia also vowed to herself to try using the happy, childlike attitude that Excella demonstrated which, she realized deep inside, was also her own.

While Celestia kept busy trying to live up to her intentions, Excella was bounding toward her destination, space station XRZ21B. Due to Excella's eagerness to get her very own clone of Lance, things were moving even faster than Celestia had anticipated. Upon reaching the space station, Excella cautiously waited for the opportune moment when she and Lance could spend an evening together. After inviting him to her suite, she carefully slipped a drug into his drink. When he reeled and fell over, sinking into oblivion, Excella extracted the needed cells and left him to sleep it off. He was none the wiser, yet thoroughly confused about what had transpired the night before. He asked Excella if they had made love, to which she simply smiled leaving him to his own conclusions. As he left her suite, still in a quandary, Excella contacted Celestia with the news that she had accomplished her goal and would, as before, meet her at the station.

Once again, Celestia played the part of the mother and met Excella for lunch and the precious vial of cells was exchanged. Excella then went back to XRZ29B without Lance ever suspecting she had left or of his part in the girls' lurid scheme.

Celestia lost no time in keeping her part of the bargain either. In a very short while, another clone would be created. Once again, when she was sure no one would be around, she repeated the process of cloning as she had done in creating Excella. At least that's what she thought. This time, however, a banging on the door of the growth accelerator startled her. This clone was not going to enter the world in such a quiet manner as Excella did.

"Let me out, let me out!" a muffled voice cried as kicking feet and banging fists slammed against the accelerator door. Celestia peered into the window and was shocked to see a frantic little boy. It was fascinating to see Lance at a very young age. Uh, oh! Celestia realized the growth accelerator wasn't calibrated properly. She wanted to watch little Lance a while longer, but fearing he might remain at that age, she re-calibrated the accelerator. At the given time, she peered through the window once more. A grown man, the exact image of Lance, stood with his arms crossed in front of his chest and a towel that Celestia had left on the chair for him was wrapped around his waist. He was obviously getting quite impatient waiting for Celestia to open the door. Celestia had no idea what the clone's reaction would be, so she was hesitant until she finally gained the courage enough to let him out.

"Where am I? What am I?" The familiar questions were repeated, in a rather impatient tone. Celestia explained about his creation, just as she did with Excella.

"You are a clone, the second Hybridite clone on earth. You were created from the cells of Lance Locke and you will be called L2. You are here to complete a very important mission."

"Mission? What mission?" The clone's impatience dwindled as he became curious. "That sounds interesting. You are extremely pretty." The clone was unaware of his innocent remark, or that his compliment was out of place.

Celestia tried not to laugh at the bungling manners of her creation. "You will be told about your mission in due time." Celestia hadn't considered the attraction her new creation would have for her, but in reflection, being just like Lance, he would naturally be attracted to her. She came to the realization that she was faced with the same problem Excella had with Lance; she felt a little sorry for how she had judged Excella so harshly. On top of that, she had an even worse problem. How could she hide L2 in her apartment and more challenging, keep him from falling in love with her? It wasn't long before Celestia was having second thoughts about how deeply she had fallen into this situation, but it was too late to do anything about it now. She would work with L2 and prepare him for his mission. The sooner they all changed places, the better! She would just have to be patient and persistent with this new clone.

CHAPTER 20

DESERT DISCOVERY

In Egyptralia, time was not moving fast enough for Alex. The days of digging in the hot sun seemed endless. He was losing patience and felt the search was all in vain. He had wanted the 'Old Ones' to be right and wondered if it was just wishful thinking that drove him on. The 'Old Ones' with their faith had admonished him, "Knock and it shall be opened, Seek and you shall find." It would be devastating to them if he were to quit now, even his crew of workers would continue their labors with uncomplaining diligence.

The latest section of the excavation had been dug to a depth of just about 20 feet when a glint of hope was in sight. One of the worker's shovels had struck something so hard he could not dig into it any further. Everyone at the dig, including Alex and Jane, scurried to the spot, excited at the prospect of uncovering something meaningful. They all worked feverishly to see what lay hidden beneath the sand.

A large wall of evenly honed stones began to be uncovered before their eager eyes. The workers were so engrossed with the discovery and the mystery before them that they kept working well into the evening. As hunger and fatigue set in, all except Alex and Jane went back to the village.

Alex tried to loosen one of the blocks of stone. By levering, pushing and pulling his efforts were eventually rewarded. First one, and then another stubborn block came loose until there was enough room to crawl through the well-earned opening. As the two entered the tunneled out cavity, Jane held a torch ahead of them so they could see. At first they were somewhat disappointed. The room was empty. Jane held the torch up higher, then lower as she and Alex walked around the room, searching for some little clue that would reveal anything about the strange, barren, underground room. Suddenly Jane stopped short. "Here, over here! It looks like a door. It blends in with the wall and is hard to see. It looks like someone tried to disguise the door to hide it." Alex hurried over to see what she had found. As he scraped away some of the plaster, several splinters of wood fell with it. He continued working until he could see the edge of the doors frame. As he broke more of the plaster off, he could tell that the wood of the door was very old. He began to kick and pull slats of wood off until the door gave way.

"The first room must have been left empty to discourage robbers," Alex surmised. On entering the secret room, they saw a wooden chest placed upon a platform. They could barely see some numbers carved on the lid of the chest, as it was covered with years of dirt and sand. Alex carefully brushed his shirtsleeve over the lid, while Jane held the torch closer so they could read what was written. The mystified couple stared in wonder as Alex traced the numbers with his finger revealing the date, 2050 A.D.

So spellbound by their extraordinary find, the couple were not aware that they were no longer alone until they heard a loud thud. Seemingly out of nowhere, a swarthy turbaned man grabbed Alex from behind and raised a knife above him, ready to plunge it into the unsuspecting archeologist's heart. Jane drew back in shock and hurled the torch at the intruder. Momentarily, the stranger was distracted and Alex wrestled loose from the intruder's grip, struggling with the man until the knife pinged onto the floor. Now down in the dirt the two men rolled over and over, punching each other with searing blows. Jane ran for the still burning torch and raised it to see Alex being pinned down. She kicked the knife over toward Alex's hand. Straining, stretching, Alex's fingers crawled toward the knife until he finally gained a firm grip on it. The knife was upright in Alex's hand when the stranger, in an attempt to obtain the knife, fell on it. The weight of his body plunged down on the erect knife and it deeply pierced into his chest cavity. Alex was stunned as he rolled the man off of him. He desperately wanted to avoid killing the man so he could question the intruder. Jane held the torch toward the mysterious man's face and warned Alex "He's still alive!" she shouted. Alex recognized him as the turbaned man that had been watching him at the festival. He was disguised with dark make-up. As the intruder gasped for air in anguish, Alex was amazed to discover that the man was Captain Marcus Marson. Marcus pleaded with Alex for mercy. In agony, straining to talk, he confessed that he had been sent by Zarno to kill him. The words slipped out of his mouth just as the knife wound brought on its fatality. Captain Marcus Marson laid in a pool of blood . . . he was dead!

The ordeal was almost too much for Jane. She had managed to keep her wits about her during the struggle, but now she began shaking uncontrollably. Alex tenderly drew her near, comforting her. "It's over now, Jane, everything will be alright now." He soothed her compassionately as he brushed her disheveled hair away from her dirt smudged, tear-stained face.

As Alex and Jane had just regained their composure another man suddenly attacked out of the darkness as if coming out of thin-air. Jane screamed "Look out, Alex!" Alex quickly spun around facing the new intruder; this time he had the advantage. He wrestled him to the floor and held the knife to the man's throat. "Now you can tell me who you are and what you want!" Alex demanded, pushing the knife closer to the terrified man's neck.

"Mercy" the gasping man pleaded, as he stared in horror at the dead body on the floor. "I'll tell you, if. . . if you'll just move that knife away." Alex drew the knife back from the trembling man's neck, but still held him fast.

"The authorities, some Hybridites . . . they wanted me to follow you in case you found anything important. They want to destroy anything that you might find."

"Anything? What do you mean by anything?" Alex pushed the knife closer to the stammering stranger's throat once again.

"Please . . . I'll tell you all I know if you'll spare me," the man continued, pleading in desperation for fear of ending up like the dead man, lying on the floor in front of him.

"All right, out with it; and don't spare any details or I'll not spare you!" Alex threatened the man as he also looked at the body of Marcus to emphasize that he meant it.

"I . . . I live in the hills." The frightened man stammered as he began his explanation while pointing to the doorway, toward the hills. He continued explaining, "I live in a cave up in the hills with my wife and children. A stranger bribed me with food and blankets and other things for my family. We are poor and we barely get along, but I didn't take his bribe. He started asking questions about you and your search in the desert and when I refused to help him, he said my wife and children would be killed if I didn't cooperate and do as he wished."

"Yes, yes, go on!" Alex prompted. "Why did they choose you to find out about me?"

"Well, they found out that I was nearby and overheard that man talking with another man from a place called . . . uh . . . Cal . . .Calif . . . or, oh, California Island! That's what he called it! He said they must confi . . . confis . . ."

Alex finished the word for the obviously uneducated man. "Confiscate?"

"Yes, confiscate any information or anything found by you that might cause trouble for the government. They have already destroyed much that was found before. I heard those men talking. They said there was a civilization buried from a huge cata . . . cata . . ." The man's eyes grew big with wonder as Alex again finished the word for him. "Cataclysm?"

"Yes, that's what they said, they said they had to destroy everything or we Barbarians would rise up and get out of control."

"What else? What else did the men say?" Alex again prodded.

"They said that their scientists are going to predict the end of the world. They said that this would be done so they would have a reason to rid the earth of so many people . . . something about a black hole and being over-populated. They weren't talking about people here. They were talking about the Hybridites; their own people. They would send them into space, but the people here, they would be made slaves. Do you think that's true? Do you really think they can make slaves out of us? No, we'll hide. We won't be slaves! They can't make us, can they?" The man rambled on. He was out of his wits from fear and did not know what to believe.

"So that's it! I knew they were up to no good! You can go! Go back to your family and don't say anything to anyone about what you've heard or what you've seen." Keeping his promise to spare the man's life, Alex raised the knife once more so the cowering man could see that he meant what he said. "Remember, don't tell anyone about anything you've heard or seen." Relieved to be alive, the man promised he wouldn't, then hurriedly scrambled out of the ruins and fled toward the hills.

After Alex and Jane recuperated from their horrendous confrontation with Marcus Marson and the man from the hills, they turned their attention to the coveted wooden chest. Alex had already brushed the dirt and sand away; Jane held the still burning torch high so Alex could make out the roughly carved date. "The date was probably carved the year that the chest was placed here, which was probably sometime just before the cataclysm occurred. They must have seen it coming and tried to save something important, Alex surmised." "Let's see what's inside." The lid of the chest was stuck from being closed up for so many years. While struggling to pry it open, he tilted the chest back and forth. As the lid finally began to give, a small metal object rolled out into the darkness. Jane lowered the torch down and their eyes followed the sound of metal rolling over the floor until Alex was able to retrieve it. To the curious couple, the metal container's contents were a mystery. They knew nothing about the container's contents, yet they were certain it must be important or it wouldn't have been put into the chest and kept in this secret catacomb. "It's very unlikely that any Barbarian would know what this is," Alex said to Jane, as he showed it to her; "but, there is someone who might know."

"Do you mean Lance?" Jane asked.

"He might know, but he is out on a mission." Alex put the small container in his pocket and told Jane, "Celestia might also know, and she can be trusted not to tell anyone else."

The adventurous couple again gazed into the open chest again and found something wrapped in a purple velvet cloth. Alex carefully unfolded the cloth, hoping to find an answer to their mysterious treasure hunt. As he unwrapped the velvet cloth a large gold skeleton-shaped key appeared. When he held it closer to the light of the torch he figured the length of the key was about six inches and the width about two inches. Imbedded along the spine of the skeleton key were seven jewels imbedded in gold; each jewel sparkled with a color of a rainbow. Alex and Jane were puzzled. What could it mean? They thought the exquisite key might be very valuable, however it did not unlock any secrets of their past. While Alex continued examining the key, Jane noticed a piece of animal hide that had been placed under the key.

"Alex, "Look! Here's a piece of hide that was under the key. It contains a map and there's a picture of the key on the map. The key looks like it's pointing toward a Sphinx."

Alex was aware that there were pyramids and a Sphinx some distance away, on the other side of a nearby river, but no one knew what the massive structures were for, or who built them. What could be the connection, he wondered. He turned the key around several times. One of his fingers pressed a jewel and to Jane and his amazement, a tone sounded. Alex was disgusted. "Hmm, it's just a fancy musical instrument, but it might be worth something if the gold and jewels are real."

"There must be some other purpose since it's pictured with the Sphinx," Jane replied.

"Well, if that's so, I have no idea what it could be. The Sphinx is just a big rock! There's nothing special about it," Alex responded sarcastically.

Weary from the ordeal they had been through; Alex was too tired to think about it any longer. Upon leaving the catacomb the couple tied the chest onto the back of one camel and both rode on the other. Alex planned to tell the elders about Zarno's plot to kill him and to show them what he and Jane found in the morning. He didn't think they would know any more about the jeweled key or the map, but at least there would be hope that more clues of their past could be found. Exhausted, Jane leaned on Alex's back and fell asleep as he guided both camels to the village.

The next morning, Alex conferred with the elders; it was agreed that Alex should take the key and follow the map to the Sphinx. There wasn't much to go on, but there was a chance he might discover something else. Alex was skeptical, but the elders had faith that when he arrived at the Sphinx, he may just find a way to solve the mystery of their past. Although to Alex, there was a slim chance that anything would come of it, but to appease the elders once and for all, he would go. Besides, he had nothing else at this point to place his hopes on.

Jane pleaded to go along. She was eager to be included in the adventure. Alex argued that the trip across the desert in the sweltering sun would be too much for her and there was no telling what other danger they might run into. Jane continued to argue with him, and to no surprise, finally won her case. Alex reconciled himself to include her on this adventure since he realized that if she didn't go along, he would be thinking about her the entire time, anyway. As they prepared throughout the day to travel to the Sphinx, a wooden shelter with curtains was crafted to be put on the back of the camel

Jane would ride. She was excited about the adventure, and even more about being with Alex. While she packed food and other necessities, she joked about being a Queen with her entourage. Alex feigned disgust and told her the wooden shelter was just to keep her from complaining about the sun. He was not about to let her know his real thoughts. He was not about to lose control of the situation by letting her know how much he loved her. Underneath his gruff facade, he was very pleased she would be at his side.

Alex convinced two brothers, two strong men known as Bull and Bear, to accompany them on their journey. They were selected for their strength and endurance. Also, they were fierce fighters and might be needed if such an unfortunate occasion should arise. It was well known that unscrupulous, nomadic Barbarians often roamed unpopulated areas of the desert.

The little group headed out across the sands at dawn in order to take full advantage of whatever cool air was left from the night. They hadn't gone very far before they met their first challenge. One small skirmish with three robbers proved no match for Alex and the brothers. The travelers laughed about the robber's feeble attempt, especially when they came up against Bull and Bear. Proceeding on with their quest, the cool morning was giving way to the rising mid-day sun. A soft breeze was welcomed as the sun rose higher; however, the gentle breeze gradually turned into a forceful wind that soon was blasting gusts of blowing sand. They covered their faces with the cloth from their turbans to keep the sand out of their mouths and noses; only their eyes were uncovered as they struggled through the pelting sandstorm. The unforgiving wind tore the curtains off Jane's shelter sending them whipping across the desert, too fast to retrieve. The wooden frame was no longer of use on Jane's camel, so they used it and the camels as shields to huddle behind until the storm blew over. They had gone too far to go back. When able, they proceeded on, moving toward the river where there would be a safe haven among the palm trees. When they finally arrived at the river, they stopped only long enough to recuperate from the tiresome journey and allowed the camels to quench their thirst. As suspected, the river was low, so they were not worried about crossing on the camels. In spite of being tired and hungry, they decided to get to the other side before eating and resting any more. Now that the harsh winds were behind them, and after passing the lush lands by the river, it was pleasantly calm and serene. The little group had eaten and rested. Refreshed and spirits raised, they ventured on in the baking rays of the sun.

Their contentment was soon to be short-lived. In the distance small black specks began to grow larger as they trudged forward across the sand. Sooner than they would have liked, a group of swarthy turbaned men on horseback, road up and stood before them. From the richness of their clothes and ornate rigging on their horses, it was plain to see they were not poor. The apparent leader of the group trotted forward from the others and greeted Alex and their little band with a smile. "Welcome strangers! Welcome to our land on this side of the river!" Unaware of their intentions, Alex rode forward to return the greeting. It soon became obvious to all that the strangers were not going to be friendly. As Alex and the others moved forward to pass, trying to avoid any confrontation, the band of nomads started laughing. Then the band of ruffians blocked their path around them, with the leader commanding, "You cannot pass on this side of the river until you and your companions have paid a tax."

"Tax? What do you mean, tax? There is no tax and you must know we don't have any money. No one has money." Not wanting to accelerate trouble, Alex tried to keep calm.

"Well, then, we'll take your camels . . . and oh yes, we'll take the woman, too!" the leader added as he looked toward Jane. One of the men got down off his horse and started toward Jane to take her, but Jane was prepared. She had dismounted her camel and stooped down as if afraid, and cautiously grabbed a handful of sand. When the man tried to grab her, she threw the sand in his face. He was shocked just enough to give her a chance to give him a good hard kick. Then all hell broke loose. Although Alex and his group were outnumbered, they were not outsmarted. Bull grabbed two of the robbers and cracked their heads together while Bear grabbed another man, threw him over his shoulders, then turned rapidly several times hitting two others hard with the dizzy man's feet. Alex jumped in the air and gave a hard, direct kick to the belly of another man. Immediately, another grabbed Alex from behind and pinned him down in the sand. Jane quickly jumped on the aggressor's back, pulled his ears and poked her fingers in his eyes until he release his hold on Alex. The scuffling went on, until thanks mostly to Bull and Bear; the would-be robbers were either knocked senseless, or had ridden off on their horses, not wanting to ever see this small band of travelers again!

After watering and resting the camels and themselves, the little group continued on their journey, once more. As they traversed the desert the massive Sphinx came into view, looming larger and larger, until they were face to face with the gigantic man-faced stone lion. They felt very small as they stood peering up at the awesome structure. Alex carefully removed the key from its velvet cover. He had no idea what he was supposed to do with it. He pressed the jewels several times, but the Sphinx remained silent and motionless. After passing the key around, with each trying to get some result, it was finally passed to Bull. Bull held the key in his hand as if to study it for a few moments before he spoke. "I'm, well . . . I'm a musician" the hulk of a man shyly admitted. "Remember the night of the festival? I played the flute. Maybe the jewels are notes like in a song." His large hands toyed with the jewels a few times. He pressed each jewel in a caressing manner. He tenderly pressed the jewels in different combinations, searching for some sign of a connection between the key and the Sphinx. Just when the group was about to give up, Alex thought he heard a cracking sound. "Play it again, Bull." Bull tried to remember what he had played. He tried again and again, until he found the right notes that made the cracking sounds increase. Then to their amazement, there was a loud rumbling noise.

"That's it, that's it. You've found the answer, Bull!" Everyone yelled ecstatically as the rumble of a great door got louder and louder. The frightened group backed up as quickly as they could, fearing the gigantic, man-lion statue might crumble and fall on them. Instead, a door between the Sphinx's paws slowly opened. The small group's fear turned to joyful relief on finding such success. Shortly, their excitement paled back to fear when it came time to enter the massive structure. They were not nearly as brave as they thought. First, Alex hesitatingly stepped through the doorway. As the little group joined him, a torch was lit as they anticipated venturing into darkness. Instead, as if by magic, the whole place was full of light. Some of the walls were adorned with mirrors, and other walls and the pillars were encrusted with quartz that reflected the sunlight radiating from the doorway. Even more amazing was the fact that the Sphinx housed an enormous amount of objects; every kind of object imaginable. The mouths of all four members of the group dropped open as they beheld the contents of the structure. They slowly moved farther and farther thru the great-pillared halls, finding things of every description. There were household items, manikins dressed in clothing of time going back thousands of years. There were paintings and a library full of carefully cataloged scrolls, books and documents. Every conceivable thing that revealed what civilization was like before the earth had wrenched itself into chaos. They each tried to lock on to the things that would be important to tell the 'Old Ones' about when they returned to the village and create mental images in their minds. Each also carefully selected as many items they could carry to take with them. As much as the adventurers wanted to investigate more, Alex made them aware that they must leave until they could return at another time. As if waking from a dream of the past, the little group wended their way back out of the Sphinx; back into the present. Hopeful of finding the right notes on the key to close the stone doorway, Bull again pressed his fingers on the jewels. Much to everyone's relief, his musical ability again proved sufficient. The huge stone door ground back to its original position, causing the magnificent monument to be eerily austere once more.

Still in awe, the little group chatted excitedly about all they had seen. As they traveled back to the village to share their discovery, Alex confided to Jane, "We'll have to make another trip. This time we'll have to go back to Jameripan. We now have proof of our past. We have to get in touch with Celestia, so Lance can be warned. She's the only one we can trust, the only one who might be able to get in touch with him. He mustn't go on that mission and we don't have much time. We'll rest one day and the next day we'll leave at dawn. That is, of course, if you want to come along." Alex spoke as if it didn't matter to him one way or the other. Jane did not respond, yet a tiny smile at the corner of her mouth was enough of an answer. They knew without saying that they would both be in Jameripan very soon.

CHAPTER 21

A SECRET MEETING

In Egyptralia, Alex and Jane were preparing for their trip to Jameripan, where they intended to show their recent discoveries to Celestia. At the same time, Celestia was busy with her own undercover activities. She had managed to keep her secret. No one even suspected she had cloned a species any higher than an insect, much less a Hybridite. She had trained the assistants left to her according to Dr. Hall's recommendations, and felt it was now safe to leave the laboratory work in their hands. Of course she jealously guarded the serum compounds, as well as the information for the cloning of a higher species. She often had misgivings about her own use of such knowledge and felt it would be disastrous to let that kind of information out. She believed the world was not ready for that, especially without the supervision of someone like the Professor.

It was too late to undo what she had already done, and she alone would have to live with the results and accept responsibility of her actions. If only she had decided to leave her work to be with Lance before she cloned herself. Well, she reasoned, what was done was done. There was no turning back now. Celestia knew she could let the clones disintegrate, but how cruel that would be after giving them life. No, she reasoned further, she couldn't. It would be like murder! A little sneaky manipulation was one thing, but that was as far as she would go. With renewed resolve of her intentions, Celestia left the laboratory and returned to her apartment.

"I'm home!" Celestia announced. L2 was too engrossed in a computer game called Quick Wits to acknowledge her greeting. She smiled to herself as she noticed how childlike he was. He was intrigued by everything, and so eager to learn. Like a newborn, he relished every aspect of his new-found life. He yearned to explore and discover all that was around him, how things worked and interacted with other things in life.

Finally L2 became aware of Celestia's presence. "I'm glad you're here, I've missed you so much!" he confided, in his usual innocently polite manner. Celestia was also polite, but not overly friendly lest he get the wrong idea. She still had to be on guard; had to control the situation or she would have the same problem that Excella faced with Lance.

"Well, what shall we have for dinner tonight?" Celestia asked, not really expecting an answer and yet trying to keep things light-hearted. She rattled off a few ideas, which included the regular fare of sea greens and vegetables. L2 left his game playing to follow Celestia; he watched her every movement and listened to her every word, like a baby following its mother. L2 was far from being a baby, however, and sometimes he got too close for Celestia's comfort. It was difficult to keep him at arm's length, not only because of his interest in her, but she also had a hard time remembering that he was not really Lance. While Celestia busied herself, setting the table, she didn't notice just how close he was getting. She set some dishes on the table and was going to get some more. As she turned around, her eyes suddenly met his. Their eyes locked momentarily, in spite of her attempts to avoid such a confrontation. She and L2 were just too close for comfort when fortunately, the communications buzzer sounded and a picture of Alex and Jane appeared on the security screen.

Celestia hesitated before answering. "Why Alex, Jane! What are you doing here?" She was relieved to have the interruption, but was not ready for company. "What a surprise! Don't you know? Lance has already left! I'm so sorry you missed him, but when I hear from him I'll be sure to let him know you came by." Celestia became nervous; it would have been disastrous if they knew about L2. How could she hide him? She hoped Alex and Jane would be discouraged and leave, since Lance wasn't there, but that wasn't to be. Alex and Jane were not easily discouraged.

"We're right here in your complex lobby and we've got to see you right away. It's very important. It's about Lance. We can't talk here; we've got to come up!"

Celestia was beside herself. "No!" she rudely stated. Then, trying to act natural, she changed her tone. "I mean, no, not tonight. My place is such a mess with working late and all that. I'll tell you what. I'll meet you at the Liquid Revitalizing Shop next to the lobby. I haven't had dinner yet, and there isn't a thing to eat here anyway. Then we can talk and have dinner at the same time."

Celestia breathed easier when Alex agreed to her proposal saying, "Okay, we'll see you in a few minutes. Please hurry!" After quickly zapping a dinner for L2, and convincing him to eat his dinner and then play Quick Wits until she returned, she zoomed to the lobby via the transportube.

"It's so hard to believe!" Celestia didn't know what to think after hearing what her friends had to say. She was almost in shock and toyed with her meal, while across the table Alex and Jane confided to her all that had transpired since they last met. "Our government is run by crooks? How could they keep us in the dark all these years?" She would not have believed her very good friends, if they hadn't divulged the gruesome happenings of the previous days, along with proof of their discovery. She stared at one of the historical documents left by the people; the people that Alex and Jane called Human Beings; the people who had lived long ago until they were buried by a devastating cataclysm. "It's so horrible!" she gasped, "Not only for those beings, but think of all of the Hybridites up there on space stations not knowing what treacherous intentions have been planned for them. What are we going to do?"

"We can't let anyone know yet," Alex answered, "It would cause complete havoc. Everyone would panic. They'd be so angry, no telling what would happen. There surely would be a bloody revolt. But one thing's for sure, Celestia, you're going to have to stop Lance before he leaves for another planet!"

"Tell Lance by myself?" Celestia questioned helplessly, "What about you and Jane? Aren't you going too? I think I can get transfer papers for both of you. Lance won't believe me. It's all too fantastic!"

"He'll believe you when you show him this proof." Alex handed Celestia the capsule of microfilm that he had kept when he opened the chest at the dig. "There is a lot more information back at our village. Not only is there historical and religious documentation, but also reference to a famous king . . . a king called Elvis. He was worshiped by many of his subjects. There were millions of golden platters made in his honor. I guess those Human Beings were big eaters and needed a lot of platters for their banquets. We think the chest was buried in the year 2050 for safe keeping, just before the huge cataclysm occurred and destroyed their civilization. They must have known it was going to happen and wanted future generations to know about it. They wanted to leave a legacy to any survivors. They left no mention of the Hybridites, so we believe they came here to earth after the cataclysm."

"Now, as far as Jane and I are concerned, even when those evil rulers are brought to justice, we won't belong here in Jameripan. Your world might be nice to visit, but it isn't our world" Alex wrinkled his nose, emphasizing his point, as he looked down at the strange food served to Celestia. "We're going back to Egyptralia. Besides, after what happened at the dig, we might be watched. It was dangerous coming here, but we had to see you; not only for yours and Lance's sake, but for the whole Hybridite population. No one would want to be under the domination of Zarno and those . . ." Alex did not finish what he was about to say. He just looked at Celestia and shook his head. Then he looked at her more intently. "Celestia, you're our only hope! If you really love Lance, you've got to get word to him. You must get word to Lance and stop him from going on that ridiculous, insane mission!"

CHAPTER 22

DOUBLE TROUBLE

Celestia felt alone after Alex and Jane left for Egyptralia, even if L2 was with her. Not only was she alone with the fact that she had cloned two beings, but to make matters worse, she was now alone with the responsibility of getting the microfilm to Lance and coaching L2. No longer was her intended trip to XRZ29B just for her own welfare; now she was working to help save her people from the horrible plan of their own President. This was no easy task; she had such short notice, and she had promised to leave first thing in the morning. Before going back to her apartment, Celestia decided to go to the lab for one last look. She would leave a note for the assistants who were to take over upon her departure. It would tell them that she and Lance decided to get married before he had to leave on his latest mission in space. It seemed to be a perfect alibi.

The dimly lit lab was quiet as a tomb. Celestia's footsteps echoed in the silent laboratory as she thought about Dr. Hall and her long career with the happy times as well as the stressful times spent here. She smiled at pictures of the two of them during some of their special moments. She lovingly brushed her hand over some of the familiar objects, realizing it would be a long time before she might see them again. Everything was different now. Celestia wondered how she could have ever been so impatient, so eager to get away from her work. The past as she knew it was gone; her world was shattered by the news from Alex and Jane. Would there ever be a better world? The transition wouldn't be easy, but it wouldn't be caused by any foreign body crashing into the earth, as the so called President of the Honorable Order Of The Source had told them!

Celestia remembered Dr. Hall's words when she had asked what good would the knowledge of cloning a higher species do. His words came to her loud and clear, as if he were still there speaking to her.

"For science's sake!" The professor's voice seemed to ring in her ears. "Who knows why or when such knowledge might be needed!"

Celestia walked over to the information bank and flipped the switch on. She keyed in the code to bring up the secret cloning procedure. Breathing a sigh of resignation, she deleted every byte of information. It was a secret that only she would know. Now it would be left for future generations to rediscover. She then mixed enough life giving formula to give Excella and L2 their maximum life span, which was not even as long as an ordinary Barbarian. Celestia had found out what Dr. Hall had meant when he said his discovery wasn't perfected yet. He could not make the formula last for the clones indefinitely. They would die like the Barbarians who had not learned to expand their life cycle yet. Celestia thought how silly the Barbarians were to cling to their old ways. They were intelligent enough, so maybe they weren't animals after all. She shuddered, thinking of how they still reproduced like animals and how they indulged in eating meat. To her it was not only barbaric it was bizarre!

Tears emerged from Celestia's large almond shaped eyes, as she took a last look around the laboratory. She locked the door on her former life and went back to her apartment where she hoped L2 would be asleep. If so, she could prepare for the early morning trip without the interruption of his advances. Her hopes, however, were in vain. L2 was not asleep and he was feeling quite amorous.

"You're the most beautiful woman I've ever seen. Let's read minds" L2 innocently coaxed.

Celestia was aloof to his suggestions. She told L2 he was silly, for he had never seen another woman. Then she quickly changed the subject. "L2, I've got a surprise for you; it's going to be our secret. You need to meet another woman since you have never met anyone other than me. You have no one else to compare with. So, we're going on a trip and you're going to meet someone . . . someone very pretty!" Celestia enjoyed her self-complimentary statement. "I know you'll like her; she was made for you." Literally made for you, Celestia thought to herself.

"Oh, no one could take your place, Celestia. I couldn't love anyone but you!"

"That's what they all say," Celestia muttered under her breath. "Well, L2, you just wait and see. Now I have to pack, so here . . . here are some rapid assimilation tapes for you to watch if you're not sleepy." Celestia handed L2 the tapes that had been left behind by Lance titled 'Rocket Building and Space Technology for Home Study'. L2 was immediately interested and took the tapes to his room. He became so engrossed in them he forgot all about Celestia and spent most of the night watching them. The next morning, Celestia tried to rouse L2 who mumbled a few facts about rocket technology before rolling over and going back to sleep. She gave up and let him sleep a little longer, while she showered in golden rays of light. Feeling revived, she threw on her silvery robe, stepped into her matching slippers and scuffled to the kitchen while calling a little louder to L2. He finally lumbered out of bed and put on Lance's bathrobe and slippers that Celestia had set out for him. Of course there was no problem of fit. After more coaxing, he finally made it to the kitchen. Celestia thought to herself, just like Lance, I have to call him at least three times before he comes to a meal. L2 was fascinated as he watched the process of making breakfast. Celestia put three small round discs on her plate and a bigger portion of six on L2's plate. She sprinkled them with a few drops of water and zapped them with a microgun. Instantly the discs began swelling, changed shapes and finally emerged into recognizable eggs, soysages, and algae pancakes served along with cups of green revitalizing beverages. L2 was impressed with Celestia's cooking expertise. The smells of the cooked food was irresistible to him; he quickly gulped down the results of her culinary art.

After breakfast, Celestia helped L2 with his disguise. She was fortunate to have friends in the theatrical world. They were delighted when Celestia offered to buy some of the costumes they no longer had use for, and although curious, did not question her reason for purchasing them. She picked out clothes that would be perfect for her and L2 to wear. They would travel disguised as an old man and his wife. A few last minute items were packed and a public shuttle-skimmer was called to take them directly to the shuttle station. It would look too suspicious if she used her own sky-skimmer; better not to leave it parked at the shuttle station, she reasoned.

With the transfer papers in order, thanks again to 'Good Old Sam the Transfer Man' as he was called, and thanks to a second nerve-wracking trip she had suffered to get them, the journey to space station XRZ29B went smoothly, except for a few incidental hitches.

Upon their arrival, Celestia did not know where either Lance or Excella would be, so she and L2 remained in their disguises. Finding a Revitalizing Fluid Shop, they took an empty table next to a window and ordered a couple of drinks along with a snack of seaweed muffins with a sprinkling of ground ants on top. Celestia gave strict orders, telling L2 to remain at the shop while she made reservations for sleeping quarters and also to find out where Lance might be. While she was gone, L2 amused himself by again going over a manual of the Rapid Assimilation of Rocket Technology Home Study Course he had brought with him. After reading for a while, he glanced out the window to watch the people as they passed by. Suddenly, he spotted Excella and assumed it was Celestia without her disguise. He jumped up and ran after her, thinking she forgot which shop he was in. He pushed his way through the crowd of shopper's and finally caught up with her.

"Did you forget where I was?" L2 questioned the surprised Excella. He was still attired in his disguise which was unrecognizable by her. She tried to ignore him at first and kept on walking. L2 was confused as to why the supposed Celestia was ignoring him and persisted in his pursuit.

"Help!" Excella yelled, "Help!" A crowd of onlookers turned to stare at the commotion. "Get away from me, old man, stop following me!" Excella was frantic. She was oblivious to the scene they were making. In the meantime, Celestia had returned to fetch her charge.

Oh, No! I told L2 to stay right here! After making sure he was nowhere in the shop, she figured he must have been bored or curious and wandered out to look around. Upon leaving the shop, she heard the commotion and spotted a crowd gathering. It wasn't difficult to realize that the commotion was a result of L2 getting into some kind of trouble. Then she saw the clones arguing. This was a turn of events that Celestia had not bargained for. First she would have to settle the argument without making more of a scene. Then, she would have to explain the mix-up to L2 and Excella, but first she would have to get the crowd to disburse. Catching up to them, Celestia tapped L2 on the shoulder. He turned to face her with a baffled look on his face while Excella wondered what was going on.

"Hey, there are two of you!" L2 blurted. Fearing more attention, Celestia had to get the clones away from the crowd. Thinking she was being hassled by an old man and woman, Excella resisted Celestia's tactful coaxing. Celestia eventually convinced the contrary clones to return to the Revitalizing Fluid Shop peacefully, where she promised to explain everything. As Excella realized that Celestia was wearing a disguise, she willingly went along with her. As hoped, L2 obediently followed in puzzled bewilderment.

When they got back to the shop, Celestia steered the clones to a quiet booth in the corner where she recounted all that had transpired before their arrival. Excella did not expect a meeting with Lance's clone so soon. She wasn't really shy, but the actress side of her made L2 think she was. Naturally, L2 was delighted to meet Celestia's double. The cloned couple was immediately entranced by one another. Celestia's plan was materializing: She would now be able to try to make up with Lance without any interference by Excella. It soon became clear to Celestia that the clones, being enamored with one another, were ignoring her. She impatiently began to prod Excella for information on the whereabouts of Lance.

"It's become more difficult to see Lance," Excella confided. "Countdown time is almost here, and I guess you know what that means . . ." Her words drifted off, knowing that Celestia did indeed know what that meant. If she didn't get to him soon, Lance would be headed for disaster!

CHAPTER 23

AN IDENTITY CRISIS

Celestia was especially pleased that her cloning effort of L2 turned out so well, and that Excella fell in love with him immediately after he had removed his disguise. Excella could see he was made in the image and likeness of Lance. She assured Celestia there would be no problem as far as her former attraction to him was concerned. Celestia cautioned the two clones not to show they were lovers in public. She and L2 would have to continue wearing their disguises, at least for the time being.

Excella showed Celestia all she could about where Lance's reporting stations were. After looking them over, Celestia chose the one she felt would be the best to try to enter. Celestia even tried to get past the guards by pretending to be his mother. Her scheme did not work. She was turned away by the guard who told her, "You'll have to have clearance papers before I can let you through, even if you are his mother." When the guard started questioning her more about her intentions, Celestia pretended she couldn't hear well. "What? What did you say?" she repeated over and over, until the disgusted guard told her to just go away sensing there was no need for further questioning. Later, when she discussed the situation with the clones, they all tried to think of another way to get past the guards.

Celestia searched for a solution. "There's only one other possibility I can think of. L2, do you think you know enough about rocket technology to impersonate Lance?"

L2 stroked his fake beard. The more he thought about it, the more intrigued with the idea he became. Like a reckless teenager, he wanted to show off and get in on the real action. "Sure, I think I can!" he exclaimed, eagerly agreeing to try.

"Now, if you find Lance you're going to have to be sure to get him somewhere alone," Celestia warned. "Don't let anyone see you together. We'll have to wait for just the right moment, and then you'll need to remove your disguise. Excella will show us the most likely place to find him." Celestia briefed L2 as best she could. "Now remember, he doesn't know he has been cloned, so after you get to him and you are alone, reveal yourself to him and put your disguise back on. Give him this note; it will explain everything. Now L2, you must be prepared for his reaction. He will most likely be overwhelmed at first, and when he calms down let him see your face. You'll have to give him your disguise and change places with him. Assure him that it will only be for a short while so he can meet with me. Follow his directions. Let him tell you where to go, so you won't be in contact with anyone while you are taking his place."

The three impersonators carefully rehearsed their plan. Excella named and described the persons Lance worked closely with, in case L2 did come in contact with them. She gave L2 Lance's schedule, and also told him when and where he ate and slept. She drew directions to the training room and how to get to the rocket poised for outer space that loomed above them. Excella's directions were specific, like Celestia's directions would have been. "The best time to work their plan was early evening. That would be when the trainees Lance was instructing for inter-galactic travel would return to their quarters. Lance usually stays a little later than the others to prepare for the next day's work. He would be checking last minute details concerning the rocket flight equipment as a safety precaution for the first crucial moments of blast off."

Celestia was impressed with Excella's ability to coach L2 for his mission.

Excella went on with her directions. "I remember Lance explained to me that the rocket was programmed to take off at the end of a countdown. He told me there would be no possibility of cancellation once activated. After take-off, the remote controls would take over and guide him to the Pleiades. That's where it had been determined the best chance of finding an inhabitable planet would be located." When all points of the plan were covered, it was decided that Excella should take L2 to the training area by herself. It was agreed that a third person would be too obvious, so Celestia went back to her room to wait for them.

Excella led L2 to the chosen entrance. They stopped a little way before arriving at the gate and hid from view while L2 took off his disguise. L2 had to muster all the courage he could, for from that moment on, he would have to impersonate Commander Lance Locke. The two clones held each other closely, nervously searching each other's eyes. They didn't have to speak; they knew of the danger and importance of their charade. Finally L2 gently pushed Excella away. He left without looking back and bravely walked up to the guard. Since it was dark, the guard looked him over carefully while L2 struggled to maintain his composure.

"Unusual time to be out and about, isn't it Commander?" The impersonation worked; the guard thought he was Lance.

"Ahem, I'm just out for a quick date, you know how it is, it's easy to forget how late it's getting." As L2 spoke to the guard, he held his head down slightly while he looked to see if anyone else was watching. He breathed a sigh of relief when the guard simply nodded with a slight grin on his face and answered, "Yes Sir, I certainly know how that is." He opened the gate and let L2 pass through. It was too close for comfort, but at least L2 had fooled the guard. Having passed the first test, he stealthily moved around the area, searching for the training room where Lance would be preparing for the next day. On entering the designated building, two men in uniform came down the narrow hall toward him. There was nowhere to hide. L2 copied their salute and said nothing. After the men were safely by, L2 again sighed with relief. He continued working his way down the halls following the detailed directions Excella had given him. Whenever he could, he ducked behind a wall to avoid any confrontation with others. The inevitable happened however, when he saw someone approaching. There was no place to hide so L2 saluted, hoping to walk away without being questioned. He thought he was safely past them until he heard a voice call back to him.

"Commander Locke, Commander Locke! Didn't you recognize me? I'm the pilot you helped when Captain Marcus Marson was supposed to be in charge. I'm Stellar Odin. Don't you remember? Why, I'll always be grateful to you. You saved me from being court martialed!"

L2 struggled again to retain his composure. He had no idea what the young pilot was talking about. "Oh, yes, I remember now, but I'm in a hurry, can't stop to talk. Oh, uh, have to go to a meeting, you know, can't be late." L2 hoped his excuse worked. He hurried off, hoping the officer would not be suspicious and mention anything about him to Lance's superiors. Stellar, on the other hand, was abruptly left in a disappointed quandary. "Meeting? What kind of meeting could there be at this hour?" Puzzled, he scratched his head as L2 disappeared from view.

As L2 continued on his way, he wondered if he would ever find Lance. The sooner the better. That last encounter was too close for comfort. L2 finally did see Lance through the window of a doorway. Lance was busily checking a wall full of lights and dials. Fortunately, just as Excella had thought, Lance was alone. L2 pulled the old man disguise over his face. Cautiously he tried the door. To his relief it was not locked. Still cautious, he entered the room.

Lance turned and looked at L2. He was both surprised and angry upon seeing the old unbidden guest. "Yes, what is it?" he barked. "Don't you know this is confidential area? It's off limits! Do you have a pass?"

L2 was startled when he actually saw an exact likeness of himself. Because of his desire to carry out his mission successfully, he tried to keep his wits about him. In spite of his lack of confidence, he managed to speak. "I have a message for you, an urgent message."

"What message?" Lance stared skeptically at what he thought was an old man.

"Here, read this!" L2 quickly held the note out for Lance. "It's from Celestia."

"Celestia? Who are you . . . how did you get in here?" Lance demanded, still gazing intently at what he thought was an old man. He took the note and slowly read it, and then he looked up in disbelief as L2 slowly peeled off his mask.

"Well, I'll be . . ." Amazement swept over Lance's face.

L2 had hardly given Lance time to gather his senses. "I can't explain details now, you've got to trust me and change places with me. We've got to work quickly before being discovered. No telling how long I can get away with impersonating you. Here, put on this mask and go to this address." L2 pointed to the address written on the note from Celestia. "I'll stay here until everyone else is asleep before I go to your quarters. That way I'll avoid any suspicions. The less I have to talk to anyone, the better"

"But . . . but . . . how will you?" Lance started to argue and before he could finish, L2 interrupted with a surprisingly commanding voice. "We don't have time for this, Lance. It has all been worked out. Just follow the plan and don't worry about me, just go!"

Coming out of his state of shock at the whole incredible situation, Lance managed to give L2 some last minute advice on taking his place. I will return after I meet with Celestia and we will exchange places again. Then he waited for a chance to slip out, leaving his double to the mercy of his abilities, his luck and his fate.

When Lance arrived at his room, Celestia made certain it was Lance before she opened the door. When he entered, she wasn't sure she was seeing Lance or L2 in the old man disguise. When Lance saw Celestia in the old lady mask, he couldn't help laughing out loud. That cinched it. By his laughing at her she knew it was Lance, not L2. They took off their masks and laughed at each other. Their light-hearted mood quickly changed, however, when they became serious. Celestia explained all that had transpired since she had seen him, and of Alex's discovery. Lance looked over the microfilm and other evidence that Alex had given to Celestia. "This changes everything! I've got to tell those I can trust, those who will be loyal to me without arousing suspicion, until we can break the news to anyone else. Above all, we don't want people to panic when they find out their great 'President of the Honorable Order Of The Source' is a . . . a . . . damnable farce!" Lance squeezed the words out through clenched teeth. Now he would cooperate fully with Alex, Celestia and the clones. Together, they would do all they could to eradicate the evil grip that Zarno and his cohorts held on everyone. While Lance and Celestia began making plans to settle things at home, they were unaware that things were not going well for L2. When Excella arrived at the rocket facility to be with L2, one of the guards, convinced that they were Lance and Celestia, approached them.

"You're under arrest!" The words rang out to L2's and Excella's horror.

"Why? What are we being arrested for?" Excella exclaimed!

"All I know is that I've been given orders to detain you. You'll find out later, after being questioned by the authorities."

L2 knew he had to act. He couldn't risk being arrested, so he grabbed the guard and tried to take his weapon away. They tore into each other. First one seemed to have the upper hand, then the other. As they wrestled, Excella stood back not knowing what to do. She didn't want to call out for help. She was afraid it would only make more trouble and ruin their whole plan. Desperate to help L2, she worked her way toward the door, intending to run to Celestia and Lance for help. Before she reached the door, the guard grabbed Excella's ray gun. He was about to shoot L2, when someone else broke into the room. He drew out his ray gun and zapped the guard. The stunned guard fell to the floor. Excella was relieved when the intruder asked, "Are you all right, Lance?" The officer was none other than Stellar Odin, the pilot L2 had met in one of the corridors. He was the pilot who thought he was Lance, telling him how grateful he was for not disciplining him in the control room. Stellar still thought he was talking to Lance.

"Commander Locke, what is going on? Why were you and the guard fighting?"

It seemed L2 was always making up excuses. This time was no exception. First he patted Odin on the back, thanked him and told him that now they were even. Stellar stuck his chest out proudly for being able to pay back the superior officer who had helped him.

"It was nothing, sir, it was a privilege, sir." Then, Stellar asked again, "But why were you fighting, sir?"

"Top secret, Stellar, top secret. You know how important this mission is and that guard was prying, looking for top-secret information he shouldn't have been looking for. We can't be too careful. Now Stellar, I know I can trust you and I want to be able to depend on you if any more trouble arises. Can I do that?"

"Oh, yes sir, you can depend on me!" Stellar assured L2 he would cooperate, still unaware that he was not really talking to Lance. L2 did not want Stellar involved any more than possible.

"The guard is just temporarily stunned and I'll see that this situation is taken care of. In the meantime, I've got some work to do and then I have a meeting to go to. You're quick action was commendable, Stellar." L2 spoke with a commanding voice, trying to sound like Lance. He was enjoying his role of authority, even if it was only temporary. "I will see that your heroism tonight is acknowledged." L2 didn't stop to think about how Lance would react to his promise.

"Yes, sir, thank you sir!" Stellar saluted and scratched his head in wonder as he left, yet proud to have been helpful to whom he thought was Commander Lance Locke.

CHAPTER 24

AN EXPEDITION

California Island rumbled to one of the frequent earth tremors, while the president of the Honorable Order Of The Source sat behind his desk. Deviously plotting his next plan of action, Zarno ignored the rattle of the revitalizing fluid and liquor bottles, as well as other objects on his desk as they shook.

One of Zarno's cronies tried to calm the angry president. "It'll be over in a minute as usual." As he was finishing his comment, the president slammed his fist on the desk, making the objects jump again. "Damn it!" he cursed loudly, ignoring the tremor and the words of his crony, showing that his concern had nothing to do with the antics of nature. "That so and so Barbarian, Alex Carter Taylor has done it!" Zarno ground Alex's name through his teeth in seething hatred.

"Done what?" the crony questioned meekly.

"Don't you know anything? Haven't you heard? Marcus Marson has been murdered! He was supposed to get rid of that Alex fellow. You know, that Barbarian, that pest living among the rest of those outcast terra-forms in Egyptralia. He's been snooping around and apparently found something. . . a box of so-called records and all that hokum. It's a dangerous situation. He'll cause an uproar if he blabs about it to his Hybridite friends, Commander Lance Locke and Burt Rogers." Zarno emphasized Commander in a sarcastic manner. "They might believe him, so we've got to get to him before he broadcasts it all over the place. Don't you see, we'll be ruined if that kind of gossip gets spread around? Now listen! I've got a plan. We're going to have an expedition of our own, but we've got to think of a way to keep the rest of the Hybridites from knowing what's going on. After all, we don't want to cause any unnecessary commotion, do we?" The president snickered at his remark. "And I'll tell you this, we're going to blast that Alex fellow and his camel riding friends off the face of the earth!" He leaned back in his big leather chair and continued talking with a self-satisfied air. Unaware of what Lance, Celestia and the clones were doing at that time, Zarno felt confident. "Everything's going as planned up there on XRZ29B. We're going to get that Lance Locke off the space station soon, and when we get that archeologist taken care of, it'll be smooth sailing again. Well, what are you waiting for? Get some men going on this!"

"Right away, right away . . . we'll take care of Alex Taylor, don't you worry about that Mr. President." The crony tried to act in charge by covering up his fear of Zarno, but as he meekly backed out of the door, another earth tremor occurred. Windows and objects in the room rattled, causing him to shake with fright and betray his pretentious confidence.

In spite of his fears, the chastised crony gathered enough courage to confer with the others loyal to the president. He mustered an air of authority long enough to convince them of Zarno's plan. An expedition was arranged immediately, but soon afterward the poor Hybridite's conscience and fear enveloped him so much, he crashed his skyskimmer into a rocky cliff. It was declared to be an accident not a suicide, of course, and Zarno's plans were continued.

The journey to Egyptralia could not be kept secret from the Hybridites, so an announcement was broadcast that they were preparing to search for a lost civilization; just in case the word of Alex's discovery got out to the public. In the event of such a leak, it could be said that Alex's venture was a hoax made up for his own aggrandizement. It was predetermined that the eventual outcome would be that nothing was ever found. They would publicly announce to the gullible population that President Zarno and his men successfully squelched Alex's unforgivable hoax. "It would be the perfect cover-up," the devious president proudly professed.

As Zarno's airships were manned in preparation for the deadly mock expedition, word was spread among the Hybridites who were eager to hear about a lost civilization. Maybe something uncovered might help them with their present plight regarding the earth. They were still convinced that the earth was about to be smashed by a collision of a meteorite from space. Perhaps, they thought, if there was a lost civilization, the occupants must have come from another planet and there would be hope for them to return to it. The news of the expedition, supposedly dictated by the Source, made known by Zarno, ultimately reached the spaceport.

"You know what this means." Lance shook his head as he read the news. "That's no expedition; they're going after Alex! They want to get rid of him. We've got to stop them!"

"But what can we do about it?" Celestia felt the situation was hopeless.

"I'll have a crew organized in no time. Those buzzards are going to have some unexpected company!"

Zarno's men were already making plans to invade Egyptralia, as Lance busily rounded up the best and most trustworthy men under his command. When they found out the truth about the Honorable Order Of The Source and the evil president, Zarno, they were sworn to secrecy. They didn't want to alarm the general population and cause a panic. In spite of being outnumbered, they were eager to follow Lance's orders. As the men raced toward their airships, a spirit of comradeship was evident. Lance had personally seen them all off on their bold mission.

Just as he was about to join his crew for takeoff, he hesitated. He looked back at the towering rocket ship that the Hybridites had worked on so hard to perfect. Then he looked up at the sky in the direction of the Pleiades. He had felt so certain that he really would discover another inhabitable planet. If he went to help Alex, the expedition would be canceled. The rocket ship would be deserted and there would be no chance of it reaching its destination. It would be like a ghost ship that loomed above them. No one would ever know the possibilities that could have been uncovered; but there was no time to speculate. Lance had to act quickly; he had to choose. He either had to help Alex destroy the monster, Zarno, who kept everyone at his mercy, or take the chance his men could defeat Zarno without him. Then he would be free to fulfill his own intergalactic mission that he wanted so desperately to perform. It would be a glorious event. If successful, a whole new world might be opened up for his people. It would take years to duplicate the endeavor. In fact, this might be their only chance to discover another inhabitable planet. There was no time to lose. Lance started to run toward the huge craft, then, he stopped abruptly. He stood motionless, not knowing which way to go. He felt everything was happening in slow motion. Thoughts raced through his brain; thoughts of how Alex,

Jane and the rest of the Barbarians would be slaughtered at the hands of Zarno's men. He visualized the carnage that would occur. There would be no mercy, even for the women and children. He had to make a decision! Suddenly the choice became clear. As if something other than himself controlled him, a burst of energy overtook him, forcing him into action. He ran toward his own airship to join the crew that was ready and waiting for a confrontation with the enemy. He was now convinced that his true mission was right here on earth.

CHAPTER 25

TWO HEADS ARE BETTER THAN ONE

L2 drew Excella close to him as he poured his feelings out to her. "Excella, we do not have enough longevity serum to live very long. I don't want to insist you stay with me. You can go back home to Celestia. She'll take care of you. Of course, I will always love you and want you to be with me, but I will understand if you decide to leave. The trip to outer space will be dangerous and I don't know what might happen, but I want to make use of the time we have left. I want to have lived for a purpose, so I'm going to proceed with Lance's plan to go to the Pleiades. I can do anything that Lance can do."

"I only want to be with you!" Excella took L2's hand and looked lovingly up at him. "I feel as you do. I don't care what might happen, as long as we're together. We will reach for the stars!" Then, with a look and nod of mutual understanding, they both ran for the now deserted rocket. They quickly put on spacesuits and secured themselves in the pilot and co-pilot seats. L2 and Excella held hands as L2 carefully pressed the countdown activation control button. They slowly counted 10 . . . 9 . . . 8 . . . 7 . . . 6 . . . 5 . . . 4 . . . 3 . . . 2 . . . 1.

A huge burst of fiery white heat blasted beneath the massive craft; it lifted it into the air slowly at first, then gaining speed, thundering toward its destination . . . the Pleiades!

A frantic voice communicated to Lance. "Do you see what I see? Commander, my screen shows two persons took off in the rocket headed for outer space! My request for identification was ignored. No one knows who they are, sir!"

To the surprise of the communications officer, Lance laughed loudly, then cursed jokingly, "Why, those sons of Barbarians!" He looked to the sky just in time to see the rocket hurtling upward. He watched the afterburners of the craft get smaller and smaller until it disappeared out of sight. The frantic voice was still looking for an answer. After a few moments, Lance chuckled as he communicated back. "Never mind, all we can do, whoever they are, is to wish them a safe journey!" Only Lance and Celestia knew who the two pilots were. As Lance proceeded toward Egyptralia, he was concerned about L2 and Excella. He thought of the two lone brave clones hurtling through space toward an unknown destination. Spurred on by their bravery, his spirits climbed. As he neared Egyptralia he became even more determined to win the upcoming battle. He looked up at the sky and shook his fist. "Go for it!" he shouted, "Go for it!!" Then, he turned his attention to his new mission. He concentrated on intercepting the men sent by Zarno before they reached Alex and his men. By the time the first wave of his newly formed crew had reached Alex's village, Zarno's military police had already begun using their weaponry on the meagerly prepared Barbarians. They were helplessly scattering for shelter, when suddenly, diving swiftly down out of the clouds, Lance and his immediate crew entered the scene of battle, diverting the attention of the president's men away from the terrorized people below.

The final battle of airships ensued with a screaming, frightful clash of Hybridites against Hybridites, metal and fire. Zarno's men were being beaten not only by the Barbarians, but even his own subjects. Zarno's surviving Hybridites scattered, flying as fast as they could away from Egyptralia. The silence of the aftermath was even more noticeable after the burning devastation that was common to war. Alex, along with the rest of the Barbarians, ran to meet the victors. How truly grateful they were that Lance and his crew had arrived in time to thwart the evil mission of Zarno and his men. Alex and Lance had succeeded in escaping from Zarno's evil scheme. They shook hands and agreed that there may be new worlds in space; but first they would have to develop a new world right here on earth. "My mission isn't complete yet. We're going to put Zarno out of commission." Lance and his crew turned their airships toward California Island.

CHAPTER 26

THE RECKONING

President Zarno paced the floor of his office at California Island.

"Our ships are down!" a voice announced.

"Don't you think I know that?" "Don't you think I know that, you idiot?" The enraged Hybridite had been looking at his monitoring screen, watching the defeat of his men. "Lance Locke and that Alex Taylor have joined up together. Lance and his crew of rebels are on their way back here!" he fumed.

Another earth tremor began shaking the room. This time furniture slid across the room and a picture of the president fell to the floor.

"It's an earthquake!" cried one of his staff, who had been called in with other high officials to watch the battle in progress.

"Oh, don't pay any attention to that," Zarno scoffed. "It'll be over in a minute as usual. Right now we've got to get another fleet out to stop Lance and his men from coming here!"

A loud rumble was heard as a speaker announced, "Alert! Alert! Seek emergency shelter at once! I repeat . . . earthquake . . . volcano erupting . . . seek shelter." The voice trailed off in a frantic attempt to warn everyone, but the speaker, unable to keep his balance, took his own advice and ran for cover, as did the president's Heads of State.

"Where are you going? Come back here you yellow lizards! It's just a false alarm . . . It's just a little tremor! It'll be over soon . . . Don't leave me!" Zarno pathetically tried to demand the loyalty of his staff, refusing to believe the end of his evil power was inevitable. The building began shaking violently. Now the frantic president finally decided to heed the former warnings. He ran toward the door only to see hot lava flowing on the floor toward him. He ran for another door, but there too, the red-hot, molten liquid closed in on him. Closer and closer it came. He climbed up on his desk where he became trapped. As the hot liquid spewed higher he frantically raised his desk. He raised it as far as it would go, until his head was being crushed up against the ceiling. "Help! Help!" he yelled, but there was no answer. No one was there.

Lance and his crew had barely arrived within viewing distance when Zarno was pleading for help. They did not have to attack, for they were just in time to see the opulent crystal and gold building that housed the monstrous regime crumble. Flames engulfed the structure. Melting gold and crystal mingled with the molten lava. Zarno's super computer, the Source, suddenly seemed to come to life. It had never worked since Zarno and his predecessors had taken over. Zarno had pretended to be the only one capable of deciphering the messages of the so-called wisdom that he, himself professed. Now the computer suddenly began working. It was mumbling something. It got louder and clearer exclaiming "It's hot in here! It's hot in here! As it continued on like a broken record, Zarno frantically shouted, "Shut up, shut up you stupid bunch of nuts and bolts!" From the mouth of the volcano, it belched and scorched ooze, rumbling thunderously loud. The burning magma rose straight through the roof of the once magnificent building. Zarno desperately clung to his desk on top of the rising lava flow, while the Source followed him, still repeating, "It's hot in here! It's hot in here!" From a distance the horrifying sight of the explosion could be seen scattering debris from the building while the burning lava spewed in every direction. Black smoke filled the air. The Hybridites tried to scramble for safety as the whole city crumbled. Lance and his men were unable to save the innocent Hybridites or any of Zarno's men. Helplessly, they watched in horror, cringing at the extreme devastation and loss of life that they were witnessing.

The victors, awed by the sight, circled at a safe distance away. They did not have to destroy the capitol. Earth itself took revenge. Seeming to resent the evil resident there, it caused a miracle to rid itself of the unscrupulous leaders and their government. The volcano had not only devastated the capital, aftershocks affected the whole country of the Hybridites. Those who were fortunate enough to live through it would have to try to pick up the pieces the best they could. Nothing would be the same now. Why did the innocent have to suffer? What was to become of them? The stunned survivor's questions could only be answered as the future unfolded.

"Well, that's the end of Zarno and his Honorable Order Of The Source!" Lance announced to his fellow crew members. As he gave the order for them to return to their stations, their ships veered off through the spreading black smoke into the blue sky above. They quickly disappeared from view, leaving the city and Zarno's government center to smolder behind them. As they traveled away from Jameripan, they could see how widespread the volcanic activity and earth tremors affected the surrounding areas occupied by the Hybridites. What molten lava had not consumed, fires did. Now their spectacular glass and metal buildings had crumbled into smoldering ruins. The remaining Hybridites would soon realize that they would be left to the mercy of the Barbarians.

CHAPTER 27

NEW WORLDS

Most of the citizens of the Honorable Order Of The Source had never known the truth about their fallen leader or of his evil intentions, and there was no need to tell them now. As far as they were concerned, the earthquake and volcanic eruption were an unfortunate natural disaster. They were sad that it had happened and mourned the death of their leaders. They believed the expedition to Egyptralia was a success, and in a way that they did not suspect, it was. Lance announced the news in a speech to an eager listening public. "Evidence of a former civilization has been found. Not only that, but new evidence has been discovered. We have found that the earth is no longer subject to the danger of being destroyed by a meteor, for it has passed out of range of our planet." The Hybridites were told of the historical finds that Alex uncovered. Also, it was announced that from now on they should be called Human Beings rather than Barbarians, as their history revealed.

Many of the Barbarians, or Human Beings as they were now called, would have liked to kill the remaining Hybridites. They felt that way because of how they had been treated by them. Nevertheless, it was decided that they had been subjected to this unfortunate fate by Zarno's regime. Aid would be given to the innocent Hybridite survivors if they would acknowledge them as Human Beings, rather than Barbarians or animals. After the Hybridites new officials agreed, speeches were made by Alex and Lance, followed by eating and dancing until late in the evening. Eventually, Lance and Celestia left arm in arm to be by themselves. Lance confided to Celestia how he regretted not being able to complete the space mission to find other inhabitable planets.

Celestia tried to console him. "Lance, you know you did the right thing."

"I suppose you're right, Celestia. Yet, I can't help thinking about the opportunities it could have revealed. Just think of the possibilities."

Celestia tried not to show it, but she was on the verge of tears. Lance, everything will be so different now, she mourned. Our civilization is in ruins. Our beautiful buildings are gone. Our factories, shops, homes, our technology, everything is gone. I realize the Barbar . . . , Celestia caught herself. I mean the Humans . . . they will help us like they said, but it's so sad to think we will never live like we did before. If only we could find a way to get to XRZ29B. Couldn't we live there?

Lance tried his best to console Celestia, but he had to tell her the truth. "No, Celestia, we don't have any way to get to the space station, and even if we could we wouldn't have enough fuel or other means to live there. It's a vacant city now. We will have to try to make the best of things here. Anyway, we have each other."

"You're right, Lance, we have each other," Celestia agreed. "As long as we have each other, we'll get along somehow."

Celestia's attention reverted back to XRZ29B. "What do you think will happen to the space station, Lance?"

Lance thought for a moment. "Oh, I don't know; I guess it will be there for a long time. Maybe someone from another world will find it. Or maybe it will get swallowed up by a black hole, just like Zarno intended. Only this time there won't be any Hybridites on it. On the other hand, maybe it will just float around in space, like a ghost ship on the sea of eternity."

With more positive resolve, the couple turned their attention elsewhere. They wondered what had become of L2 and Excella. Were they still alive? Did they find another planet? Would they ever know? Looking up in the direction of the Pleiades, Lance saluted to their brave cloned companions. "It's a new world out there Celestia, just waiting for anyone who yearns for adventure! Perhaps the rocket mission wasn't in vain after all." The two lovers continued talking about the future possibilities for their people and themselves.

Celestia pointed to the sky. "Perhaps that is our true home up there. Maybe that's where we originally came from after all, and maybe one day all Hybridites will go back home where we really belong."

"Home! No matter where we came from, our home isn't in Egyptralia, Celestia. The Humans will let us live and I'm grateful for that. They will even give us aid, but that's not how I want to live. We must go home, back to what's left of Jameripan. There must be some biospheres left, some means of survival for us. We are not slaves and we do not want to live among the Humans. Their ways just aren't our ways, even if they mean well. No, we're going home Celestia, and I feel certain that most Hybridites will feel as I do."

"You're right Lance. Even though I have doubts about how we would survive, I too, want to go home."

Lance drew Celestia close to him. She had seemed so strong in the past; strong in that she was a capable business person, not needing anyone or anything. Now she was like a child wanting to go home. He comforted her as best he could. "It's true, it will be hard for us for a while, but we will make it. Whatever may happen, Celestia, we're going home!"

Following the lead of Lance and Celestia, most of the Hybridites returned to Jameripan. They picked up the pieces of their fallen civilization, determined to survive there as best they could.

CHAPTER 28

SPACE II

As devastation ceased rocking the lands of the Hybridites, Lance and Celestia's clones, Excella and L2, were experiencing mind shaking events of their own. They had often seen the beauty of the earth below when they were on the space station. But now it was different as the earth grew smaller and the feelings of excitement gave way to feelings of fear and sadness. They knew they could never come back home to their beautiful blue planet. Hurtling through space, beyond the space station, they had narrowly missed meteors and other debris. Days and nights passed. They took turns bolstering each other up, especially when they wondered if they would ever see another planet. A major worry was the fact that they did not have an endless supply of the life-prolonging serum. Celestia had given them all she had made and destroyed anything related to cloning. If that wasn't bad enough, their food supply was dwindling and they were getting weary as the trip continued. They decided to eat a carefully doled out portion of what little food they had left before they drifted off to sleep.

Excella was the first to awaken when the light of morning pierced the darkness. While dividing a small portion of the rationed food, she happened to look out the window. Something caught her eye. She squinted to see if there was anything that really did catch her attention. Maybe, just maybe, she thought she really had seen something. "L2, L2," she called as she shook his arm to wake him up. L2 tried to ignore her. He turned away, hoping she would let him sleep, but she persisted. Finally he arose; trying to humor her, and looked to see what she was talking about. He stared out the window momentarily. "It's your imagination Excella, just wishful thinking." L2 closed his eyes and tried to go back to sleep, but Excella still prodded him to look. L2 realized it wouldn't do any good to try to sleep, so he looked again. Upon seeing a small speck in the distance getting bigger, his disbelief gave way. Suddenly he jolted to life. "I think you're right, Excella! You are right!" he acknowledged excitedly. "It's a planet! We've done it, Excella; we've found a planet in the Pleiades, just like we hoped we would! Maybe there's life on that planet; maybe there's hope for us!" The two clones were ecstatic and full of questions. "Do you think there is life on the planet?" "If there is life, what would they be like?" "Do you think they would be friendly?" "Would they let us land?" It seemed there was no end to the questions that they were eager, yet afraid, to have answered. At first L2 was too excited to eat the meager portion of food Excella had given him. After the initial excitement, he calmed down and devoured his ration. Then his attention turned to the matter of getting close enough to the planet to make a safe landing. They still had some distance to go, and fortunately their rocket ship was performing well. Everything was under control, so they tried to relax as much as possible while cruising toward the unfamiliar world. As the planet became larger, L2 went over everything in his mind that he had learned from the accelerated rocket training course. Celestia had given it to him when she wanted to keep him busy. He had learned what he needed to know when he took over the rocket they were in. Now, it really came in handy. When L2 felt they were close enough to descend, he released the rover module they occupied from the rocket, reversed the position of the module, and they glided gently down to the planet's surface.

Once safely landed, the couple fastened on their space helmets before L2 retracted the metal cover from the glass canopy. "It certainly looks barren," L2 noted.

"I see what you mean," Excella agreed. "Looks like nothing but sand and rocks. Well, no time like the present. Let's get out and look around."

"You're right, no time like the present." L2 opened the door slightly to make sure their suits were strong enough to withstand the atmosphere, in case it was too hot or too cold. After a few moments he climbed out of the module, then, cautiously felt the ground beneath his feet. "It seems all right. Come on Excella, we'll walk around a little. Maybe we'll find some sign of life here." Excella joined him and as they walked a little way from the module, L2 kicked some rocks. He was disappointed and angry. "Damn it! There's nothing here but sand and rocks. We've come all this way and there's nothing here. It's a dead planet!"

"Look! See? There is someone here. There are several beings and they're coming from behind those big rocks!" Excella exclaimed. "They're coming toward us." She grabbed L2's arm and clung to him as the beings came closer. Both L2 and Excella had their extermination guns attached to their space suits, but dared not use them unless they had to.

L2 squinted his eyes to see better. "I can't tell if they're real beings, or some kind of robots that look like beings. They have some kind of insignia on their sleeves; they must be from a military force or something official."

Excella couldn't tell either, but no matter what, their only choice was to do their bidding. The native occupants surrounded the couple and motioned for them to follow. They walked some distance before they came to a gigantic bubble looming before them. The bubble was so transparent they would not have known it existed, except some strange creatures flew toward it, flopped themselves against it and slid falling off to the ground. The clones' escorts, whether beings or machines, somehow walked right thru the bubble taking the clones with them. As they entered, it became clear that there were other beings in the bubble. Some of the residents had gathered to see the strange visitors approaching.

"They're aliens!" they cried, "They're from outer space!" others cried, pointing their fingers at the frightened clones. The uniformed escorts paid no attention to the panic stricken populace. While they continued leading the captive clones to an unknown destination, the couple saw more of the strange beings flopping against the bubble as if trying to get in.

"I guess that's why they have the bubble. They want to keep unwanted pests out," L2 told Excella. Even if the guards could understand them, they did not offer an explanation.

As the group continued on, L2 and Excella were amazed at the difference in the surroundings from where they started. There were all sorts of trees, lush grass, flowers, pathways and fountains. Peacocks roamed the grounds and swans gracefully glided over lakes, just like at California Island. In fact, everything seemed even more colorful. After some distance they entered a spectacularly beautiful building.

To L2 and Excella, it was an architectural wonder. Upon entering, they were led to a large open area with tall pillars. They couldn't tell if the pillars were made of highly polished metal, glass, or crystal. The walls looked like they were made of stained glass in all of the colors of the rainbow. The floors looked like cold, hard, shiny marble, but to the contrary, they were soft and warm to walk on. A sparkling chandelier of silver and gold with glistening crystal prisms hung from a high colored glass ceiling. The effect was as if one was on the inside of a kaleidoscope. A red carpet led up seven steps where the clones stood before a beautiful lady sitting on a throne. On each side of her there were two ladies, all beautiful and elegantly attired. At the back and sides of the room, guards stood at attention. They were apparently ready to make a move toward the strangers if there was any sign of trouble. Bugles with blue flags decorated with dolphins sounded to announce the arrival of the strangers. Poised, sitting with perfect posture, the lady was a stately, undoubtedly royal figure. Silky waves of golden blonde hair framed the strong, yet gentle features of her face. Her skin was flawless, with a hint of suntan, as if she had just come in off of a palm lined beach. Her figure was enveloped in a low cut aqua-blue gown. It clung to her as if part of her perfectly proportioned body, revealing ample rounded breasts, slim waist and firm hips. A gold medallion embellished with the image of a diamond studded dolphin hung from her neck along with several strands of pearls. Her gown flowed over her well-formed torso, legs and ankles. It seemed she might be a mermaid, but her gold sandals with sea colored stones along a center strap, proved that she wasn't. To complete the vision of loveliness, and make no doubt as to her royal status, the queen held in her hand a scepter; a long gold staff with a golden dolphin at the top. An exquisite crown with seven sparkling diamonds, representing the seven stars of the Pleiades, rested on her head. As

L2 and Excella drew closer, it was difficult to keep from staring at her sea-blue eyes. Suddenly their speechless daze was broken as a distinguished looking man in a highly decorated uniform approached. With much fanfare, he formally announced the clone's arrival to the Queen.

"You are in the presence of her Royal Highness, Queen Aquariana, Queen of the Pleiades." He started to continue the introduction, but Queen Aquariana motioned for him to stop. There was complete silence for a moment; then the Queen pointed her scepter up toward the crystal chandelier. As she did so, the chandelier began glowing brighter and brighter. It was so bright the frightened clones had to cover their eyes. It was even more frightening to them when the chandelier began vibrating violently. L2 and Excella held onto each other, fearing the chandelier might come crashing down upon them at any moment. When the vibrations finally stopped, the room darkened and a hologram, showing the sky with stars and planets moving in their orbits, appeared accompanied by the song Aquarius. The sights and sounds so filled the room that it was as if they stood in the middle of the universe. The clones were entranced at the awesome sight until the vision disappeared and the Queen spoke.

"Welcome to the Pleiades and the lands of the seven stars! Tell me your names, where you are from, and why you are here."

The clones hesitated, then Excella nudged L2, urging him to speak. "We're from a planet called earth," he began. "We are Hybridites. Our people were becoming overpopulated and needed to find another planet to occupy. We thought if we came up to the Pleiades we might find one that is inhabitable for our species."

"Do you mean your people intend to invade us?" Queen Aquariana questioned. "And what do you mean you came up to the Pleiades? Our planet is called Nebulon and everyone knows your planet earth is up, not ours. But then, of course, shrugging as she spoke, that is only a matter of viewpoint, because the fact is, in reality there is no up or down."

L2 hesitated again, thinking about what she said. Then, he and Excella answered together, "Oh no, we don't intend to invade you," L2 continued explaining. "My name is L2 and this is Excella. We have no intentions of invading you. You see, we are clones of two other Hybridites. We don't have long to live, because we don't have enough life-preserving serum to survive much longer. I came from the cell of a Hybridite who was supposed to go on this mission to find a suitable planet for our growing population. Instead he decided to help save the earth from the domination of a cruel and ruthless dictator, so he wasn't able to go on his mission. The rocket was all prepared for the mission, so Excella and I decided to use it ourselves. After all, we didn't have long to live anyway. It would be a terrible shame if we couldn't come up to the Pleiades and see if there was a place for the Hybridites to go to."

Queen Aquariana corrected L2. "I told you Earth is up, not the Pleiades and especially not our planet, Nebulon."

"I'm sorry, I forgot," L2 apologized, and then quickly changed the subject. "Can you tell me how it is you speak our language, your royal highness?"

"Certainly I can tell you. You will no doubt be surprised to hear our ancestors were Hybridites."

"Your ancestors were Hybridites?" L2 and Excella looked at each other in disbelief.

"Yes. We have evolved over a long period of time and we have continually improved. That's why we look better than you do." The clones were taken back by her uncomplimentary comment, but

Queen Aquariana continued as if it didn't matter. "In fact, we are also part human." That statement really threw the clones. "You see," Aquariana went on, "our ancestors were human beings at one time. They experimented and many became Hybridites like you. Most of them weren't happy with the results, however, so we combined both the qualities of the Hybridites and the Humans. Since then we have perfected ourselves even more, and there is no telling how much more wonderful we will become in the future." She spoke so matter-of-factly, as if no one would doubt the truth of what she said.

Although L2 and Excella were insulted when the Queen said her people looked better than the Hybridites, even if it was true, they were amazed by Aquariana's insensitive insult. L2 realized he was not in a position to argue. Undaunted and curious, he asked the Queen about the creatures that were flopping themselves against the bubble that surrounded them. He also asked if the Nebulons felt too confined, being surrounded by the bubble.

"Oh, the bubble isn't confining to us," the Queen explained. "We can come and go as we please, just as if the bubble wasn't there. The creatures you saw are called Ogelies. The bubble is real to them, but not to us. The Ogelies hate us, because we have everything. They're looking in to see what we have. They are trying to get in and take everything from us. They will flop against the bubble until they simply give up or die."

L2 was puzzled. "Can't they have anything? We weren't crazy about the Barbarians, but we at least gave them donations and our cast-offs."

Queen Aquariana was beginning to get a little impatient as she tried to make L2 understand. "Of course they can have anything. They just don't want anything. They want everything! They want everything we have, even though they can have anything they want.

If they had anything, they could have everything . . . like we do, but they just don't want anything. They want everything before they have anything, see? It's just not possible!"

Aquariana's explanation was making L2 dizzy with confusion, but not wanting to press the subject, he simply replied, "I guess I'll have to think about that for a while."

Queen Aquariana quickly shot back sharply, adding to L2s confusion. "Well, don't just think about anything, think about everything if you're going to think about anything at all, because you certainly shouldn't want to leave anything out."

L2 was tired of trying to keep up with what the Queen was talking about, so he resumed their previous conversation. The clones told Aquariana everything that had transpired on earth up until the time they left. They told her about the evil ruler Zarno and his government, how he used a computer-like device called the Source. L2 explained "As far as anyone knew and as Zarno professed, he alone had the knowledge to decipher the information it divulged. He had inherited his knowledge and his place as the supreme ruler from his ancestors. None of the Hybridites knew anything different, so Zarno's reign was just accepted as normal, the way it was."

"A long time ago we had a device that we called the Source, too," Queen Aquariana revealed.

L2 and Excella were surprised. "You mean there's more than one Source?"

"Yes, it didn't actually tell us what to do. It was a super-computer coded by the most intelligent scholars we had at the time. We don't use one anymore because we found it could be very dangerous. If someone who wasn't intelligent enough to use it properly, the Source might take advantage of us and take over. Besides, we now always know what we need to know when we have the need to know what we need to know."

L2 and Excella shook their heads trying to figure out what Queen Aquariana had just said. Here we go again, L2 thought to himself.

Queen Aquariana continued, "Many years ago a group of Hybridites went on a tour of the universe. They took a Source with them on their journey. Their Source must have mal-functioned, and we lost track of them. Apparently, they landed on earth and either couldn't get back or they decided to stay. That President Zarno you talked about had to pretend to have the ability to decode information from the Source. That way he could have power over the all of the Hybridites. The Hybridites that are on the earth must return to Nebulon. We will have to send a scouting party to bring them back. They do not belong on earth; the earth belongs to the Humans. The Hybridites will be brought back to Nebulon where they came from. However, they will have to live on our brother planet, Circulon, for they are not ready to live as we do."

"Your brother planet?" L2 questioned.

"Yes, each of the seven sister stars has a companion planet, so we call them brother planets."

L2 and Excella didn't know about the plight of the Hybridites from the time that they had left earth, so they asked, "But the Hybridites are overpopulating earth; aren't you afraid they will over-populate Circulon and then come to Nebulon and take over here as well?"

Queen Aquariana felt compassion for the clones and tried to break the news to them as gently as possible. "I'm sorry to have to tell you this, but after you left earth, there was a great volcanic eruption. It devastated the Hybridite's cities on earth and most of the Hybridites perished along with Zarno and his evil regime. Even though the Hybridites had no need to find another planet, they now know that it is self-defeating to reproduce so many Hybridites simply because it is so easy to do."

Horrified at the thought of what the Queen had just told them, the clones threw their hands up, covering their faces. "Oh, how dreadful!" Hoping that wasn't true, L2 and Excella asked, "How do you know this?"

"I didn't know what I needed to know, until I needed to know, and then I knew that I needed to know what I needed to know. So, of course I now know what I needed to know and as a result, I know the condition of the earthly beings, see?" Queen Aquariana tilted her head and raised her eyebrows questioningly. She was certain that she was being perfectly and understandably clear to L2 and Excella.

L2 and Excella didn't see. They just looked at each other and shrugged their shoulders. They knew it would be futile to question the Queen further. Queen Aquariana sensed their quandary and tried to alleviate any misunderstanding. All of a sudden L2 and Excella were shocked to watch the Queen's face and hair suddenly disappear. Her head spun around and around so fast, none of her features were visible. When her head stopped spinning, her whole head was covered with eyes; there were too many eyes to count. L2 and Excella watched in amazement as all of the eyes were looking around in every direction. It was the strangest thing the clones had ever seen. After a few moments, the eyes closed and the Queen's head spun around in the opposite direction. When it stopped, her face and hair reappeared. "You under developed Hybridites have large eyes, but you see very little. I have many eyes and I can see everything. Also, having many eyes makes it easier to back out of a parking place when the lots are crowded." The clones rolled their eyes and smirked as if disgusted. "Very funny!" they said in unison, but inwardly the clones were pleased that the Queen was not beyond expressing a little humor.

After her little joke, the Queen quickly became serious again.

"Now do you see?" The Queen saw that they still didn't see. "Haven't you ever heard of remote viewing?"

"Remote viewing?" The poor clones were too puzzled at what they had seen and heard to respond.

Queen Aquariana sensed the clones' exasperation, so she changed the subject and continued explaining her plan for the future of the remaining earthly Hybridites. "Our more highly developed people will not accept the Hybridites into our society. The Hybridites will have to develop over much time before they would be able to live with us, and they probably won't even live that long. You see, they never developed beyond their technological capabilities like we did. Nevertheless, they are like our ancestors and we will take care of them."

Before the Queen finished speaking, Excella starting swaying to and fro. She grabbed L2's arm so she wouldn't fall. L2 realized Excella was about to faint. "She's hungry. We haven't had much to eat, because we had to ration our food."

"Then we must dine at once!" The queen motioned for her attendants to prepare a meal. "We will eat in the garden. I'm sorry we don't have any life-prolonging serum to give you. Many years ago we gave up cloning; we found that it caused too much trouble."

"We can relate to that!" L2 commented under his breath. "We are very sorry to hear it, but we understand." They were sadly disappointed and hung their heads, yet tried to remain positive. L2 wanted the Queen to know that he and Excella understood her concern. "Anyway, we are glad to hear you will help the Hybridites on earth."

L2 and Excella were expecting to have a small dinner in the garden alone with Queen Aquariana. They were quite surprised when they sat down at a huge banquet table under a white pergola. Above them, the pergola was covered with varied pink and red bougainvillea along with purple wisteria. The table was exquisitely decorated and the clones were happy to see that their own kind of food was being served to them. It looked more delicious than any they had ever seen. Queen Aquariana introduced the clones to the many Nebulons seated at the table. To the clone's surprise, every one of the dinner guests had the title of prince or princess.

"You see," the Queen explained, "everyone here is a prince or princess, a title we have given ourselves in order to have the power to rule. We take turns sitting on the throne in the great hall and today it is my turn to rule as Queen." "Then," she added with a slight twinge of sarcasm, "As I told you, we are highly developed." L2 and Excella thought Queen Aquariana had more confidence than anyone actually ever needed.

The clones noticed that all of the Nebulons were dressed in different kinds of clothing; in fact, their clothes seemed more like costumes. Excella asked hopefully, "Are the guests going to be in a play?"

"No, they're just dressed to be what they want to be today," Aquariana replied as if that was perfectly normal.

"We are all wearing clothes for what we choose to be today. Another today I might decide to be an artist, or maybe I'll be an engineer, a circus performer or even a famous lawyer. I'm not quite sure yet; it seems like it's always today, so I'll wait and see what I want to be when it's another today. I used to want to be different things in the past, but it was always today so I never became any of those things yesterday, and I could never get to tomorrow either."

At that point, the clones gave up trying to sort out any sense in what was being said. Is it always today here, they wondered to each other. Are there no yesterdays or tomorrows here on Nebulon? Come to think about it, what about yesterdays and tomorrows back on earth? Are there only todays? L2 and Excella decided not to think about it anymore, lest they go insane.

The smell of baked caterpillar pie made L2 hungrier than ever. He scooped a good helping on his fork and lifted it toward his mouth when he noticed the Nebulons bowing their heads in prayer. Being embarrassed for not waiting until the others started eating, he and Excella sheepishly bowed their heads, too. They hardly paid attention to what was being said until they heard them say, ". . .and give us today our daily everything."

Excella elbowed L2 in his side and whispered, "That sounds awfully greedy."

The heavy set man sitting next to Excella overheard her. "Greedy?" he said rather loudly. He raised his hands and repeated "Greedy?" even louder, then laughed heartily. "Why ask for anything when you can ask for everything. Since we already have everything, it would be senseless to ask for anything. It only stands to reason we should ask for everything every day. Then, he let out an even bigger guffaw as all of the guests joined in the laughter; everyone except Queen Aquariana. She muffled her laughter under her napkin, since she felt it her duty to be dignified. L2 and Excella were embarrassed again, but eventually their pouty faces melted into grins. Just as if the sun broke through, they too joined in the laughter. They thought maybe there was some sense in what the overly large man said after all.

When everyone had their fill, all of the guests left, but Queen Aquariana lingered so she could give directions to L2 and Excella.

"I am going to leave you now, but you must stay here in the garden."

It was becoming obvious that the clones were beginning to fade. They were so caught up in their experience on Nebulon with the Queen and the others; they almost forgot their inevitable demise. The Queen, however, had not forgotten their dilemma.

"You must remain in the garden, but do not despair." She spoke in such a soothing manner, the clones wondered if she was really aware of their desperate plight until she continued to explain. "You won't die little ones, you will only change. After all, change is the only reality. Just like the raindrops, they change, they dissipate, and though you don't see the raindrops anymore, you know that whatever they were is still there, just different. Look, there's a bench beyond the fountain. Go, sit down and watch the water droplets rise and fall, rise and fall, again and again. There is nothing to fear little clones, and you will find it very peaceful there." She spoke so softly, she sounded almost like she was singing a lullaby.

"Are we up in heaven?" Excella asked.

"Don't you remember? I told you there is no up or down." Then, Queen Aquariana gave what she thought was a simple explanation. "To you, up or down is wherever you are. For all you know, you could be looking up when you are looking down, or you could be looking down when you are looking up. It's just a matter of perspective."

L2 and Excella didn't think her explanation was simple. They were amazed at how Queen Aquariana was so sensible and caring at times, and so strangely complicated at other times. Nevertheless, they tried not to think about her answer and did her bidding. They turned to look at the waterfall and strained to see the park bench. When they turned back to acknowledge seeing the bench, Queen Aquariana was not to be found. There was nothing else for them to do, so they walked to the fountain, sat on the bench and watched the droplets rise and fall, just as the Queen had told them to do.

As they continued watching, the clones began fading more noticeably. "Don't look at me," Excella cried to L2. "Please don't look at me!"

"It's all right," L2 comforted Excella. "I'm fading, too. Look, Excella, see? There's a beautiful rainbow shining over the fountain!" Not knowing exactly what was happening to them, the clones hung onto each other. When they faded almost completely, they had returned to their original state, back to being cells from Lance's and Celestia's bodies. A light breeze gently picked up the little cells and blew them onto the petals of some forget-me-nots. Lost to anyone's view, they seemed to disappear, and like the tiny forget-me-not flowers, they would never be forgotten.

CHAPTER 29

LOST BUT NOT FORGOTTEN

Queen Aquariana had not forgotten her promise to bring the Hybridites back to their real home. The scattered, homeless Hybridites were gradually gathered together and taken up by the Nebulons' universal tour ships. The ships were advanced versions of the one that accidentally landed on earth many years ago. It happened that many years ago, unable to get the stranded ship back to Nebulon with its malfunctioning Source; the passengers were destined to remain on the earth. At that time, the captain and officers of the stranded ship decided to imitate the Source in order to keep the frightened passengers from panicking. Even though their intentions were honorable, the Source was handed down from one generation to another and eventually came into the hands of the evil ruler, Zarno. Now that Zarno and the cities of his rule were gone, and the Nebulons knew the Hybridites had been stranded on earth, the Hybridites could be brought back to their original home of Nebulon. Gradually small groups of Hybridites were sucked up, as if in a vacuum. They would board space ships that would take them to Nebulon and eventually to Nebulons brother planet, Circulon. The

Hybridites that were not yet taken up, were too concerned about surviving to notice what was happening to others. The humans were no longer in contact with the Hybridites except for humanitarian purposes. The newly named Humans were preoccupied with rebuilding their civilization since finding out about their past in the great sphinx museum. Memories of the Hybridites gradually faded from the consciousness of the Humans. Since there was no longer contact with them, they assumed the Hybridites had left the earth to live on their space ships, such as XRZ29B.

Before that time, however, long before so many years had passed, when Lance and Celestia were still on earth, they had taken it upon themselves to help the Hybridites survive the outcome of Zarno's fallen empire. One exceptionally beautiful day, Lance and Celestia decided to go on a picnic. Celestia packed a picnic basket and they headed for a nice spot near the edge of a sparkling stream. Lance spread a blanket on the ground while Celestia brought out cricket salad, grasshopper sandwiches and revitalizing drinks. They had hardly finished the last bites of lunch when Lance noticed gusts of wind kicking up; they gathered their belongings and headed for a nearby shelter. They thought they were hearing thunder and would be caught in the rain. Lance looked up at the sky thinking he would see clouds, but instead he had to shield his eyes from the sun. "That's funny, the sky is clear," he said.

Celestia noticed something peculiar, too. "Something's pressing against me and it's not the wind. It's pulling me up!" Celestia cried. "My feet won't touch the ground!"

"It's pulling me up, too," Lance yelled. "What the . . ." Lance and Celestia were almost frightened out of their wits, but soon after they began rising, no matter how hard they struggled to stay awake, they fell asleep. When they awoke, they were so far from the earth they couldn't see it anymore; instead, before them was a wondrous sight. They beheld a gigantic space cruise ship. It was a magnificent structure lit from one end to the other like a gigantic jewel. As they gaped in awe at the spectacle, a ramp lowered toward them. They were rushed forward by an unseen force that gently pushed them up the ramp onto the deck. They stood on the deck of the ship for a few moments before a woman in a crisp blue and white naval uniform approached them. When she was close enough, the woman's face and hair disappeared just as it did when L2 and Excella watched the amazing spectacle. The stewardess's head was covered all around with eyes. Her head spun around so fast it was a blur, but when her head stopped spinning, her face and hair returned. Before Lance and Celestia regained their senses the strange woman spoke.

"I am Aquariana, head stewardess assigned to meet you today on this magnificent ship, the Colossus. I have you on the passenger list as Lance Locke and Celestia Stevens."

"Yes, but what is happening, and how do you know our names?"

Aquariana answered casually, "You are being evacuated from the earth, and I know your names, because I know what I need to know when I need to know what I need to know. Haven't you ever heard of remote viewing?" Aquariana asked them the same way she had asked the clones, and also not really expecting an answer.

Lance and Celestia looked at each other questioningly. "She talks in riddles," Lance whispered to Celestia. Celestia didn't dare say anything, and nodded in agreement.

Aquariana was aware of Lance's comment, but paid no attention and continued briefing them. "The captain of this ship knows all about you and the unselfish things you have done for your fellow

Hybridites. Everything will be explained to you later at dinner. In the meantime, you will be taken to your cabins to freshen up." Before Aquariana summoned someone to escort the couple to their rooms, she pinned a welcoming bouquet of forget-me-nots to Celestia's collar. Lance and Celestia thanked her and began asking more questions. Aquariana just smiled and continued her duty as the ship's hostess.

"You will not be seeing me on this trip again. I have other work to do on another today. I will have to return by space shuttle to Nebulon." Then without another word, she left Lance and Celestia in a state of wonderment about the crisp, yet kindly manner of the stewardess.

"What do you think she meant by another today?" Celestia questioned.

"I don't know," Lance answered, shaking his head. "She certainly was an unusual lady."

Before dinner, Lance and Celestia were given a small tour of the ship. It was too massive to see very much of it. While on the tour they noticed that the ship was slicing through space at a tremendous speed. Even so, it seemed as if they were floating effortlessly, smoothly, like any cruise ship on earth moving through a calm ocean. At dinner it was explained to them, and the other Hybridites that had also arrived, why they were taken on board the ship and how they will live on the planet Circulon. They were told about how their ancestors were lost while on a space tour. The space voyager's captain and crew were worried that the passengers would panic if they knew that the Source did not work anymore. They lied to them and told them the Source was still working, when in fact; they were speaking for the Source. Rulership came down to Zarno from one generation to another. By the time it came to him, the people didn't know anything different, and so, accepted his rulership as normal. Over time, Zarno's ancestors were powerful and by the time Zarno inherited the rulership, he had become greedy and corrupt.

The newly arrived Hybridites were sad that they had been deceived by Zarno, yet delighted to know they would be safely back where they belonged, back at their original home in the Pleiades.

Later that evening, Lance and Celestia walked on the deck of the ship and chatted about all they had heard. Feeling romantic, Lance drew Celestia close. As they embraced, the bouquet of forget-me-nots was pressed between them. They were completely unaware that the tiny cells, L2 and Excella, were on the flowers. The former clones hugged and promised to see each other again. They covered snickers of laughter as the cell that became L2 jumped off a petal onto Lance and the cell that became Excella jumped off another petal onto Celestia. "We're home, too!" they professed in tiny voices unheard by Lance and Celestia. The little cells were at last content to be back to their original state.

The Colossus sailed on while passengers enjoyed the sights of space and the various amenities of a touring ship. Covered areas of the ship housed trees, flowers and other vegetation that surrounded swimming pools, casual dining, and entertainment areas. Also, like earthly tour ships, there were spas, theaters and beautifully decorated dining rooms.

Since they were no longer fearful, Lance and Celestia enjoyed a couple of days lounging about and seeing the sights. One day, while they were eating a casual lunch, the ship seemed to be leaning slightly from one side to another. Not easily alarmed, they and the other passengers sitting nearby continued eating and chatting as usual. As it became more noticeable that the ship was rocking back and forth, an announcement was heard from the captain. "We have run into some trouble, but we should have everything under control shortly. Please don't be alarmed and continue your activities. We will alert you if there is any further news."

Lance and Celestia were lingering over their hot revitalizing fluid drinks when they heard an alarm, and then a very loud warning blast sounded throughout the ship, followed by a horrific announcement. "Do not panic. Go quietly to your emergency stations. Again, do not panic. Go quietly to your emergency stations." Loud thunderous sounds and crashing noises were heard. It sounded like something was hitting the ship. Passengers were beginning to get frantic. Another announcement was heard. "Passengers seek safety immediately and crew members, report to your stations with military equipment." Lance and Celestia were herded to the emergency stations along with other passengers. They were almost separated as they were pushed and shoved along amid the crowds. They both made it to safety and were relieved to find each other again before the doors were locked. No sooner were they inside the emergency station when still another announcement was made. "We are being invaded by pirates!" When Lance heard that, he tried desperately to join the fight with the crew members. To his dismay, he was locked in and there was no one to let him out. He yelled and banged on the door, but it was useless.

Celestia tried to console Lance; she knew how desperately he wanted to help fight off the pirates. "Those who are in this room, the old, as well as the children and others who are frightened, need our help too, Lance. If you fight and get killed, you won't be a help to anyone and to tell the truth even though it might be selfish of me, I need you." Lance finally realized it was no use. He took Celestia's hand and meekly said, "I'll do what I can."

Outside of the emergency stations, passengers who had not yet made it to safety screamed and scurried for shelter as pirate hovercrafts surrounded the Colossus. The hovercrafts were above and below the ship. From both directions they blasted the vessel with deadly rays and other destructive weapons. Pirates in black spacesuits with skull and bones insignias on them were lowered onto the decks while some climbed up the sides, entering passenger rooms and killing those who had not yet left for security areas. Screams were heard everywhere. The merciless pirates were like bugs infesting the ship, hiding in corners, ready to jump out at crew and passengers alike with deadly weapons. There was bedlam as the fearsome pirates fought their way with swords emitting deadly rays. The crew members fought back with disintegrating ray guns and fired missiles at the hovercrafts. When the pirates were hit, they would tumble helplessly into space. Missiles fired from the pirate's hovercraft started fires on the ship. Trees burned, falling on metal and glass, causing both pirates and crew members to be crushed if they could not scramble out of the way. The fighting seemed endless. The pirates appeared to have the upper hand at first, but the crew members, although exhausted, were convinced they could win. When the pirates that were still alive realized they were beaten, they fled and the remaining hovercrafts disappeared out of sight.

Although the pirates were gone and the passengers were let out of the emergency stations, the ship was in disastrous condition. Many, both passengers and crew, had lost relatives or friends and they dealt with their loss as best they could. Everyone was grateful to be alive and most passengers were more than willing to help where they could. Although relieved that the fighting had ceased, it soon became apparent that the struggle for survival was not over yet. The Colossus had taken a terrible beating and was swaying and creaking more than ever. The ship was beginning to spin out of control. Another announcement was made. "If there is anyone on board who has had experience commanding any kind of space ship, please report to the command post immediately!" Lance and Celestia were just coming out of the emergency station when they heard the announcement.

"Celestia, you go back to our room and relax before you try to get involved with helping the survivors or clean up any debris. The pirates have been driven off, but there seems to be some other trouble. I must report to the command post."

"Lance, what can you do there? You don't have any experience with the more advanced technologies on this ship. After all, XRZ29B may have been much larger than this ship, but the technology here is so much more advanced, maybe hundreds or even thousands of years ahead of ours. Come back to the room with me and get some rest before we try to help."

"No, there might be something I can do; I'm going to report as requested. The ship is beginning to flounder and if there is anything I can do, I must try!" Lance held Celestia close for a moment, and then he turned and hurried toward the command post. When he got to the doorway, he bumped into another passenger who was also hurrying to report.

"Commander Locke! I'm Stellar Odin," he exclaimed excitedly. "Do you remember me?"

Lance was puzzled for a moment, and then he did remember. "Oh, yes, you were that pilot on the space station when Captain Marson left his post." He was surprised to see that not only was Stellar more mature, he too, was also a commander. The two men proceeded to find out why they had been called; it soon became obvious, for upon entering the room, they saw dead pirates lying on the floor. The ship's captain and high ranking pilots were also dead. Two crew members tried to explain the reason for the call to Lance and Stellar. "We are desperate for anyone who might be able to get this ship back under control. You surely can see that we are in a dire situation. We have no one left who can save this ship."

Lance and Stellar looked at each other in disbelief. Lance was first to admit their lack of current knowledge. "But we are not familiar with your advanced technology! Your advancements are way out ahead of ours."

"Just try," one of the crew members coaxed. "Look at everything; see if anything looks familiar to either of you. We have no other hope. What is there to lose if we're all going to die?"

With no other alternative, Lance and Stellar looked over the controls; it seemed hopeless. Stellar pointed to a large monitor screen. "Do you have any kind of operational guides to show on this screen?"

"Yes, we have a program called Quick Wits. It's been updated from an old version used a long time ago. It's an earlier version of what we use now. No one has bothered to look at it for a long time."

Stellar wasn't ready to give up. "Hey, maybe we can find out something from that. We already know the old version and we might be able to find something we can use out of this one."

Lance was still skeptical. Although not wanting to give up easily either, he examined the system with Stellar. "Well, even if we can understand any of it, it's impossible to watch and work with the controls at the same time."

"Well, maybe one of us can read out loud, look for important directions or anything helpful, while the other operates the controls." Stellar pointed out possibilities attempting a last ditch hopefulness.

"We can give it a try." Lance agreed.

Stellar started to take the seat at the monitor, but Lance had a different idea. "No, you take the controls, Stellar. I've had my turn at the controls. This time it can be up to you. If we get out of this alive, you will be the hero."

A grin crossed Stellar's face as he took the captains seat, and then the two commanders got down to the business of trying to get the ship under control. There was much trial and error along with Hybridite style of cursing, but they kept on. Lance dictated directions while Stellar applied them. Eventually the ship began responding to their efforts.

"We're going to do it!" Stellar shouted, "We're going to stabilize this monster!" Lance and the ship's crew members were ecstatic and joined Stellar in cheering and shouting, "We're going to make it!"

When it was clear that the ship was truly on a regular course, it was returned to auto-cruise status. Hearing the commotion, a crowd had gathered outside of the command post. When they were sure of the news, Lance and Stellar were taken out among the crowd where they were hailed as heroes. As Stellar was touted as the one at the controls, Lance shook Stellar's hand in front of the crowd, and then raised it high to confirm that he was the real hero. "Welcome to the club" Lance quietly told Stellar as the young commander grinned and proudly accepted the crowd's acknowledgment of him as their hero.

Celestia had joined the celebrating crowd and rushed up to Lance. She hugged and kissed him saying, "Stellar might be a hero today, but you will always be my hero." Later, at a calmer time, Celestia was curious about the pirates. "Lance, do you know anything about the pirates? Where did they come from? What did they want?"

"I didn't have a chance to find out much about them, but I did hear they are rebels from several planets. They just aimlessly wander around in space with no special purpose. When they see another space craft, they try to capture it to live on, since they have no home of their own. They don't seem to care about anything or anyone."

"What a terrible life that must be." Celestia almost wished she hadn't asked.

When the Colossus landed at Circulon, the Hybridites disembarked to make new lives on their new home planet. Lance and Celestia were given positions of high rank because of their unselfish work on earth and Lance's part in saving the ship. They married and combined their best qualities to produce one child, a son they named Excelance. Besides raising their son, the couple devoted the rest of their lives as officials of Circulon, helping other Hybridites, as well as each other.

Gradually, and eventually, all of the Hybridites did leave the earth. They migrated first to the existing space stations where they were picked up and ferried by the thousands on space ships to live in the Pleiades. There they could forget their past on earth and the evil President Zarno and his government, The Honorable Order Of The Source. Lance and Celestia happily lived out their lives in the Pleiades, feeling as if they had finally come home. Before their lives were over, they were honored as two of the greatest Hybridites that ever lived. Their son, Excelance, had been sent to school where he was educated. He eventually graduated from the Nebulon University with honors. He grew to manhood, and with the combined qualities of his parents, he became the most handsome, strong and wisest man in the Pleiades.

CHAPTER 30

THE FUTURE

In a small desert village, another couple embraced under a starlit sky. "It's a new world Jane, a new beginning," Alex professed dreamily. "We have the records of our ancestors and a civilization of people just like us. Now we know that we are Human Beings, not Barbarians, and certainly not animals. We have knowledge from our ancestors; we can learn from them and rebuild our world. We are no longer slaves ruled by the Hybridites. The wise 'Old Ones' were right. We were on the earth before the Hybridites, and now that Zarno's evil government is gone, we are free to lift our heads up high. We will build homes, shops, and cities of our own!" Alex was so entranced with his thoughts of the future, he almost forgot about Jane. She hadn't noticed for she was immersed in her own thoughts. Now that things were settled, she anticipated hearing the words she had been waiting so long for from Alex. She wondered about their future. She leaned against him, pressed her lips against his, and then looked earnestly into his eyes. "We are the future, Alex!" Alex held her close; he agreed that they were the future, yet he was not speaking of the future that she was thinking of.

The earth was still being shaken from time to time with shock waves, after effects of the turbulence in Jameripan. Now that the Hybridites had all left the earth, they no longer needed the transportube, so it fell into disuse. The Humans took what they could use from it to rebuild their civilization. Parts were used to build a new museum to house the most important items they could move from beneath the Sphinx. The key used to unlock the huge rock door was becoming worn and difficult to use. The people worried that one day they might not be able to open or close it at all. The people worked in groups to move the most treasured items before the huge stone door was closed forever. Now that digging for lost history was no longer needed, Alex and Jane worked together to categorize the contents of the museum.

One evening, when Alex was amorously on the brink of proposing marriage to Jane, he caught himself confessing his feelings about wanting to have a family with a grandmother who would read stories to his children. When Jane realized his reluctance to marry her, especially his reason, she grew tired of waiting. Leo had never given up his pursuit of her, so she finally gave in to him. Wedding plans were arranged and before long guests filled the little church. Leo stood before the preacher with bridesmaids and groomsmen beside him. The organ, rescued from beneath the Sphinx, sounded so loudly it seemed the walls would shatter. The bridal attendants smiled and tried to hold their flowers steady while the guests strained to see the bride. Leo stood with his chest out like a proud conqueror, smugly gloating about his victory over his rival, Alex. As Jane nervously started down the aisle toward the preacher, she had a queasy feeling of regret. Although Leo was not her first choice, it was time to get settled. Together they would make a home; a home she never had.

Alex stayed in his cabin. He tried to ignore the wedding. The more he tried to ignore it, the more upset he got until he could stand it no longer. Suddenly, the guests gasped as Alex burst into the chapel, rushed down the aisle and picked Jane up over his shoulder. "You can't marry that Dumbo!" he yelled. It all happened so quickly, Leo was too shocked to do anything, while Jane screamed, "Let me down you brute! All you want is a grandmother!" She shrieked profanity as she kicked and beat him on his back with her fists. The guests looked at each other in horror and disbelief. "Did you hear that?" one woman cried so loudly everyone could hear, "He wants to marry a grandmother!"

Leo stood with his mouth open in helpless shock; he was so highly insulted, his face turned red with anger. He was about to go after Alex until he noticed one of the bridesmaids smiling and looking at him with admiration. Leo's anger subsided. He moved toward the bridesmaid; she took his arm, the organist took the cue, and the wedding continued. Leo and the bridesmaid were married, to the delight of the guests who did not want to be deprived of such an occasion. Of course Jane was inwardly delighted when Alex broke into the ceremony and captured, or rather rescued her from marrying Leo. Alex and Jane soon married. Jane was especially happy, and although Alex was content and loved Jane, deep down he still regretted the fact that their future children would not have a grandmother.

One especially pleasant day Alex and Jane were invited to have lunch in the village with some friends. It was sunny, but not too hot, and cooled by a gentle breeze. They sat at a table outside of a café. As they were enjoying their lunch, a wondrous event occurred. A traveling group arrived in the village. They were not just ordinary travelers. They were exquisitely dressed. Their camels, horses and carriages were finer than any the villagers had ever seen. The visitors looked like royalty, accompanied by a large entourage. Alex and Jane were fascinated, as were the other villagers. "Who were these strangers and why were they here?" they wondered. Everyone watched in awe as the traveler's caravan finally came to a halt. A well-dressed man, who obviously was their spokesman, came forward. "We wish to speak to your highest official," he announced with authority.

One of the villagers rushed to the meeting house to get someone to come out and meet the strangers. Three of the village elders complied. "What do you want, why are you here in our little village?" they inquired. Even before the travelers' spokesman could speak, from a most ornate carriage a curtain was drawn open. A well-dressed woman motioned for one of the workers to help her. "Quickly, help me down out of here," she ordered. "Come on. . . you come too," She prompted her reluctant husband to come down out of the carriage also. They approached the elders and the woman began to explain their visit with a strange Italvanian accent. "I am Duchessa Filomena Delphina and this isa my husband the Dukea Benaldo. We have traveled very far from Italivania. Many years agoa, my brother and his wife came to thisa country. They were captured by robbers, taken away to another country and were never seen againa. The robbersa were finally captured after many years. They confessed that the couple they robbed had a little girla, but the little girla ran away and wasa left behind to fend for herselfa. We have justa recently heard that the little girla might still be alive, so we have come in hopes ofa finding her. We havea become very wealthy by making ofa the vino. As you can see, we have many barrels ofa the vino and many valuables that we can trade for other thingsa. We have everything except a familya. None of our relatives are living, and now that we have enough goodsa, we are searching for our little lost niecea."

One of the elders responded. "How can we help you? I am quite sure that the girl would be grown up by now. How could you recognize her even if she were alive?"

"We willa be the judge of thata, if you will only allow us to see your younga maidens. Our niecea, she would be abouta twenty-three years of agea."

The elders murmured between themselves. They agreed the wealth the travelers brought would be a welcomed boon to their village. "Summon the maidens between the ages of twenty and twenty-five," they announced. The maidens, of course, were more than willing to present themselves to the wealthy couple.

The Duchessa walked up and down the line of maidens to search for one who might resemble what she could remember of her little lost niece. When the Dukea saw that the Duchessa could not recognize any of the maidens, he drew a small piece of leather from his pocket, gave it to his wife and whispered in her ear. She nodded in agreement, and then walked along the line of girls again. She was about to give up her search, when Jane turned to greet the friends she and Alex were to meet. As Jane's long brown curls fell over her shoulder, the Duchessa saw the mark on the back of her shoulder. The Duchesses' eyes grew big. She could hardly contain herself with excitement. Waving her hands frantically, she beckoned the Dukea to come and look with her. When they got near Jane to get a closer look, Jane drew back. She was so startled by the strangers looking her over, she started to get up to leave. Alex, however, convinced her to let them look at the mark as a gesture of courtesy. "After all," he reasoned, "it won't do any harm." Amazingly, the mark on the piece of leather and the mark on Jane's shoulder were an exact match. Waving her hands again, the Duchessa exclaimed happily, "You are my niecea! Your name is not Jane; you are Angelica Alessia, my brother's daughter. Come, we havea brought a husband from Italvania for you!" The Duchessa waved her black lace fan, summoning the man she had chosen for her niece to marry. "This is Antonio, he will makea the fine husband for you.

"But Duchessa, I am already married," Jane exclaimed. "This is my husband, Alex."

"Married? The Duchessa drew back waving her fan frantically. "Who is this man you area married to? He looksa English." Her comment was obviously not complementary as she looked Alex up and down critically. "You musta get an annulment! Antonio will makea the better husband for you."

Hearing that, Jane was so angry she reverted to speaking like the Duchessa. "But I lovea Alex! You can keep your vino and fancy goodsa," she stomped and shouted, waving her hands at the Duchessa in true Italvanian fashion.

Alex was pleased to hear the words in defense of him, but he was shocked by her speech. "Jane, I didn't know you spoke Italvanian!"

Jane held her hands out in true Italvanian fashion as she answered, "Well, no one would listen to me when I spoke Italvanian . . . so I didn't."

Upon realizing it was futile to expect her niece to give Alex up, the Duchessa waved her black lace fan at Antonio. Like throwing a fish back into the water, the Duchessa calmly stated, "We won't needa you anymore, Antonio!" At first Antonio's face fell in disappointment; he was anxious to have the beautiful niece of the wealthy couple for a wife. He soon became aware, however, that he might have the choice of any of the lovely maidens that were enamored with him, a tall dark-haired and handsome Italvanian.

The Duchessa continued, "Now that I see that you will not leave this,. . . thisa Alex, and even though he isa English, not Italivanian, he is at leasta strong and healthy. You will have many children. We likea the big familya!"

Alex tried not to make a fuss regarding the slur the Duchessa made about him. He wanted to be amiable for Jane's sake, so he sheepishly mumbled a comment, "Well, I might someday like to have a boy."

"And I woulda like a girla," Jane added.

"A boy and a girla?" the Duchessa retorted. "You willa not have a boy and a girla! You will have five boysa and five girlsa! We likea the biga familya!" The Duchessa repeated loudly, with emphasis on the "biga."

Hearing the Duchesses' demand, Alex slunk back in his chair as if in a defeated daze; he knew it would be useless to argue. He would do anything to please Jane, or rather Angelica as her true name was revealed, for he certainly did not want an annulment. Besides, he reasoned, their children would have a grandmother to read stories to them, after all. Since everything was agreed and settled, the Duchessa ordered the musicians to play their instruments while the workers brought out barrels of wine for all of the villagers. Everyone danced and drank the wine, while the musicians played and the Italvanians sang their hearts out, as only the Italvanians could do.

Many of the hired Italvanians stayed and made their homes in Egyptralia. With the help of the Italvanians, a great estate was built for the Dukea and Duchessa, and the whole village prospered to the delight of the people. Alex and Angelica were also provided with a beautiful new home where they raised six children. Of course the Duchessa read many stories to the children until they were old enough to help Alex and Angelica work in the museum.

As the years passed, even after the lifetimes of Alex and Angelica, (formerly called Jane and often Plain Jane) the villages became towns and towns became cities. People combined their talents of every sort and along with progress in education, agriculture and technology, a great civilization emerged; it was equal to or even surpassed those whose memories were housed in the great museum of Egyptralia. The few remaining vestiges of the Hybridites disintegrated, leaving very little remnants of a forgotten civilization. As even more years passed, memories of the Hybridites faded altogether from the consciousness of mankind. Even Jameripan and Egyptralia were thought of as only mythological places in the tales told of the past. Many tectonic shifts, as well as earthquakes and floods caused upheavals so powerful that the continents moved, causing the configuration of the earth to completely change again. Civilizations rose, fell and new ones rose and fell again and again. Survivors wondered about the remnants of the fallen cities. Were catastrophes caused only by the earth itself, or by tumultuous atomic warfare? They wondered who were the people who lived then, where did they go and how? What became of them? As new civilizations emerged, populations grew and humanity spread over the earth. Territories became countries and with the expansion of countries, wars became a way of life. Then, with the advancement of technology, there came an even greater dependence on war. War provided jobs and improved technologies. With improved technology the universe began to appear accessible and mankind began to probe space.

People looked up at the stars and wondered if there was life anywhere else in the universe. Every now and then someone would say they saw lights in the sky, or they would claim they saw an unidentified flying object, or a UFO. Some people believed the claims they heard, but others would think the people who made these claims were crazy. Perhaps someday they would find out. They would go to the Moon, maybe Mars and maybe even beyond. How far they might go was yet to be known. Maybe they would even go up to the Pleiades, to the lands of the seven stars! Or should it be said, they would go down to the Pleiades? As Queen Aquariana once said, "It depends on your perspective." Oh never mind. Whichever way, up or down, it's something to think about. And what about the future? With all of their advancements, the question remains. Will mankind outlive their technology?

THE END

AUTHOR'S BIOGRAPHY

I was born and raised in St. Louis, Missouri, the youngest of seven children in a family with artistic leanings. Growing up in post-depression days, money for toys to fulfill childhood fantasy was rare; so much was left to one's own imagination. The library was a great source of entertainment for me and my siblings. I remember my mother saying "If any of the neighbors wanted books from the library, they would have to come to our house to get them."

After high school I attended the University of Missouri in Columbia for one year before I married the father of our three children. A few years later, as a single parent, I worked in offices and sold real estate. I did make time to attend classes at the St. Louis Community College at Meramec, where I received an Associate Degree in Liberal Arts. I continued on with college and eventually earned a Bachelor Degree from Webster University. The core of my education at Webster was centered on Literature in Popular Culture and its Political Implications, which included science fiction.

My children are grown and have families of their own. I have been remarried for several years and live with my husband in Chesterfield, Missouri. My writing had been put on hold during years of working and raising children. Recently, as I was going through excess papers, I came across some of the stories and poems that I had written. My interest in writing was revived and I decided to finish this science fiction piece titled HOOTS.

Besides writing I enjoy painting, decorating, travel, gardening, television movies and programs that include history or science. I endeavor to create interesting works that hold a reader's attention from beginning to end. I sincerely hope you enjoy reading this science fiction adventure.

Martha Lanser